SHENANIGANS

Jade C. Jamison

SHENANIGANS

Conor Hammond is desperate.

Well, not quite—but desperate enough to do something potentially stupid. His high school reunion is right around the corner and, now that he's a wealthy business owner, all those girls who used to diss him will want to hit on him—and he needs a buffer. His assistant Morgan Tredway's going to help out by playing his fiancée for the weekend.

But then Conor notices how nice Morgan's legs look in those red heels…and Morgan remembers how she used to have a crush on her boss. That doesn't stop them from telling themselves that these shenanigans are just distractions. It'll be back to business as usual come Monday morning.

Except the emotions feel real.

When Conor's propositioned by the ultimate trophy girlfriend and Morgan's ex comes crawling back to her, will they look back on their weekend romance as just a fling or seal the deal?

Copyright

PROLOGUE

CONOR HAMMOND HAD been laughing so hard, his belly ached. He'd thought a bachelor party would be the stupidest, most boring waste of time ever, but he'd been wrong. Prior to the event, he'd conjured up images of nonstop drinking, skanky strippers, and ridiculous shenanigans—but he should have known better. The best man, lawyer Brock Ford—formerly a good friend from his undergrad days—was also in his thirties, working, and serious about his future.

In other words, they were both mature, ensuring no *adolescent* antics.

However, that didn't mean they weren't going to have fun. As a nod to the good ol' days, the small party of few men occurred at a small bar where said men nursed beers while shooting pool and talking. And Brock entertained them all with one story after another.

While Conor was enjoying himself, he found Brock's behavior strange—because Brock had been hardnosed and serious ever since passing the bar years ago. Conor wondered if Brock had loosened up now that he owned one-third of the law firm his father had given to him and his brothers or if it was his lovely wife-to-be who'd helped the guy relax a little. Whatever the case, Conor was damn near having to wipe tears off his face from laughing his ass off.

"So the guy said to the cop, 'I don't suppose you've got one more bed for the night?'"

All three men started laughing again at the punchline to his joke and Abel, the youngest of the group, slapped Brock on the shoulder. "You're killin' me, man."

"That means you need another beer." Brock waved his hand in the air for the cocktail waitress' attention. "Or maybe you've had way too much. Hell if I know."

"If you're doing it right, you only have one bachelor party," Conor said. "So what's one more beer?"

"Indeed."

Harrison, the blond, leaned over the table to line up a shot while the waitress brought a tray with four more frosty mugs. Brock thanked her before telling his friends to drink up.

"So," Conor said, guzzling half the mug, "I thought you and I were going to be bachelors forever. What gives, man?"

Brock smiled, and it emphasized his dimples. "When you find the right woman, Conor, you don't question. You just do it."

The smirk on Conor's face belied what he really thought. "But I recall a good friend of mine telling me that you don't put yourself in a situation you'll regret later. 'In the wrong situation,' he said, 'you could wind up with a permanent disease, or you might end up a father, or even married. So fucking pay attention and keep your heart out of it'."

"I said *that*?"

Conor rolled his chocolate-brown eyes and shook his head. "She must have seduced you. You've lost your mind."

Brock got ready to speak when Abel said, "Yeah, I got that lecture from Brock before, too."

Harrison made the shot and then stood up straight. "Me, too. What gives?"

Conor thought by that point that Brock knew he wasn't getting out of this one. "It's a long story, guys…"

Conor, hoping he appeared casual, ran his fingers through his earthy brown hair and said, "We've got all night and hardly a plan. I think this is a need-to-know basis."

The other two men walked around the pool table and Conor turned, leaning over to make a shot. He sunk the remaining stripe in the pocket before turning. "Since the game's over, there's no better time like the present."

Brock grinned. "All right, guys, but you've got to heed my warning. Don't try this at home. You'll regret it."

"Regret what?"

"Just give me a minute, and I'll tell you how it all happened." The men put their cue sticks up and walked over to an empty table. Once they'd settled in, Brock said, "It's easier than I ever would have thought to pull the wool over people's eyes, so over the past few months, I've wondered more than once if people are completely stupid or if I'm just one of the best actors you've ever met."

Conor shook his head, grinning from ear to ear. "Getting pretty deep in here, my man."

Brock laughed. "Okay...so I meant what I said in the past—that I'd planned to be a perpetual bachelor...but what I'm going to tell you *now* is that when you find the right woman, all that shit goes flying out the window. I promise you I wasn't looking for a girlfriend, much less a wife. But, as you know, dad was getting ready to hand over the reins of the firm to me and my brothers—and he'd always hinted that he would only give the firm to married men. Husbands, he said, were more reliable, more trustworthy, more apt to work their asses off, etc."

"That sounds like bullshit."

"Yeah, but try telling that to the old man. I think he just wanted grandchildren so my mom would shut up about it. Anyway, I sensed that Bret and Brandon were going to take advantage of my marital status—"

"Or lack thereof."

Brock chuckled again. "Yes, *or lack thereof* at my dad's retirement announcement party...so I decided to level the playing field." Lifting his mug, he took a swallow of the cold yellow ale. "I found the cutest new lawyer in our firm and made her a proposal."

Abel said, "No way."

Brock nodded, a grin plastered on his face.

"So your marriage is a sham?"

"No...but our engagement was."

Conor polished off his beer, slamming the mug on the table. Maybe he'd imbibed a little too much. "Explain."

The charm oozed off Brock, one of his natural traits—one Conor admired and envied. "Bear in mind, I was feeling pressured. But I made a deal with Erica: in exchange for playing my fiancée, she'd get to start handling cases—her *own* cases—instead of doing grunt work, which is something we sometimes made new recruits

3

do. You know, kind of pay their dues for a while. But the way it was going to work was, when dad handed the firm over to us, Erica could walk away—from me, at any rate. She could keep the sweet new job and even the rock on her ring finger."

Harrison broke the awed silence—well, *almost* silence. It *was* a bar, after all. "So why the hell are you going through with the wedding? What changed your mind?"

"Erica. I got too close. I fell in love with her—and her family. And we have enough in common to keep us comfortable but enough differences to keep things exciting. The chemistry is off the charts, my friends, and I decided months ago that I want my kids to look like her."

Conor pretended to rib his friend. "He's got it bad, boys."

"No kidding. Guess we have to learn from the master what *not* to do."

Conor began laughing again. "You should have taken your own advice, my friend."

"No," Brock said, and Conor couldn't mistake the dreamy look in the lawyer's eyes. "I got *lucky*. I found the perfect woman in spite of my stupid self."

Conor's smile didn't fade, but he still believed his friend had swallowed the Kool-Aid, cup and all…and Conor would *never* do that. He wasn't a sucker—and women were good for one thing only. *One* thing—and if you left before morning, you would never make a mistake. Brock had admitted his error—getting too close. Conor would never do that—and he most definitely wouldn't do something foolish like playing a sexy, sweet woman's fiancé. No way in hell.

It would be a recipe for disaster.

CHAPTER ONE

IN FRUSTRATION, MORGAN Tredway ran her long, slender fingers, complete with nails painted in fuchsia, through her dark shoulder-length tresses. If other women envied Morgan, it was for her thick wavy hair—but she'd never imagined herself to be envied by other females and she didn't give a shit anyway. If anyone marched to the beat of her own drummer, it was this woman, and half the time, even the drummer didn't know what the hell she was doing—and that was a-okay with her.

One would think, with this lackadaisical attitude, that Morgan would have had a difficult time maintaining employment for a successful, wealthy business owner. But she hadn't. Instead, she'd simply had to become creative—and organized. She'd been artful in her answers for her interview five years ago and, when Conor had offered her the job, she'd realized pretty damn quick that she'd have to actually *do* all the things she'd claimed to be good at—like organization, time management, and using her people skills. She read everything online she could get her hands on and discovered quickly that the most important thing that would save her bacon was her daily to-do list. And so she'd make a list daily—as well as one she would create for her boss (that, regretfully, was often at odds at the list he'd made for himself, so she started making him an itinerary, letting him know about his upcoming appointments and meetings). Her list drove her work daily, helping her get things done and making her appear to be a lot more in control than she actually was.

At first, she'd been a pretender. Today, she really was her boss' right-hand woman.

On this particular day, however, she would have preferred to have been anywhere but work. Well, this afternoon, at any rate. She'd had lunch with her boyfriend Rex like she had many times before…except this time the asshole had decided to break up with her then and there—for no good reason.

"Why the hell do you wear so much red, Morgan?"

She'd set her sandwich down. Until the bite of his words, she'd been looking around the park, enjoying the sound of the birds chirping and the sensation of the gentle cool breeze on her calves. Something about his tone got her attention. "What the fuck does that even mean? And why do you care, T?"

Yes…one of her many affectionate names for the son of a bitch was *T-Rex*.

"You wear it too much. Have you ever considered the message you're sending by wearing it as much as you do?"

"What the hell?" She refrained from picking the sandwich up and tossing it at him. "Red is the color of confidence and assuredness." Okay, so the last word felt awkward on her tongue, but she kept going. "It's a fucking power color. And I don't like what you're saying. You're implying I don't pay attention to the clothes I put on."

Rex was already packing up his food, placing the sandwich wrappers in the plastic grocery bag he'd brought it in. "No, I think you do—and it says a lot about you."

Repeating her earlier sentiment, she raised her voice. "What do you mean?"

"I mean…I don't think we should see each other anymore."

Even though she believed him, she started laughing. "You're joking, right?" Of course, he wasn't joking—but he should have been.

"No. I'm serious, Morgan. I just don't think we're compatible. It's not because you wear a lot of red but what it symbolizes." He stood. "I hope we can be friends."

Here it came—the part of her that couldn't be contained by a tame to-do list or the conservative clothing she'd crammed in her wardrobe so she could be respectable on the job. "Does the red symbolize *this*?" She stuck both middle fingers up, making the knuckles on her index and ring fingers bend, just like she'd learned in middle school. When she was super angry, she'd add those balls to the dicks when she was flipping people off. Total anger meant the whole package.

Asshole.

"Actually—"

"Fuck you. I don't want to be friends with somebody who can't even properly explain what he means."

"I can ex—"

"Get the hell out of here, Rex." Morgan was trying way too hard to think of a play on her old affectionate nickname Sexy Rexy, but nothing came to mind. Instead, as he stood and turned, she took one jab. "You weren't that good in bed anyway."

He looked back at her. "Really, Morgan? I thought you were more mature than that."

"Well, ya thought wrong. Get the fuck out of my face before I—do something I'll regret." Yeah. As in something even less mature.

So the breakup, plus her less-than-classy way of dealing with the shock, was weighing heavily on her mind and, of course, that was when Conor called her into his office. It didn't matter what he needed; she wasn't ready for it.

But she didn't have much choice. Her lunch break was over and he paid her well for her time, attention, and work. So she told him she'd be right there and stood, drawing a deep breath into her lungs before grabbing a notepad and heading to his office.

First, though, she glanced down at his to-do list and felt at least a small sense of satisfaction that he'd completed all his tasks for the day—so at least she wouldn't have to nag him about that.

As usual, he was on his phone. For some reason, Conor always thought his time was more valuable than his assistant's. Technically, it *was*…but that didn't change the fact that she thought it was ruder than hell. More than once, she'd asked him to call her in when he was *ready*, not five minutes before.

Right now, though, she was replaying lunch in her head, so it really didn't matter where she spent her non-productive time.

"I'll get to work on that this week. I'll be in touch by Monday." When Conor hung up the phone after saying goodbye, he didn't even look at Morgan. Instead, he was tapping on his computer, possibly typing notes from the conversation he just had. As was his usual MO, he switched gears, assuming she'd keep up.

Ordinarily, she could run circles around him. Today, though, he had no idea she was not in the right place emotionally. "So I have a bit of a dilemma—and a solution, but I need you to be in agreement with it."

Okay...this sounded weird. "What are you talking about, Conor?"

He cocked a beautiful brown eyebrow and glanced to the left of the computer screen to look at her. Maybe he *could* sense her distress, because he stopped tapping on the keyboard and sighed. "Did you go to your ten-year high school reunion?"

"Why the hell would I go to a high school reunion?" Before he could reply, she said, "They were big enough dickwads the first time around. I'd only go back if my therapist said I needed exposure therapy."

Conor's eyes crinkled at the corners but she could tell he had a lot on his mind—as usual. "I'm considering going to my twenty-year."

"*Twenty?* Oh, my God. I forgot how ancient you are."

"I'm *not* ancient, Morgan. I'm not even forty yet."

"Well...if you're pushing forty—*which you are*—you'd just as well have one foot in your grave."

Conor's right eyebrow arched. "Forty's the new dead?"

Dammit. Conor never failed to make her smile, even when her mood was shit. "Do I wear too much red?"

"Is this a trick question?"

She needed to talk about it, but she couldn't bear looking her boss in the eye, so she began pacing. "You know T-Rex?"

"The dinosaur? Not personally. I'm not *that* old."

Huffing, she looked over at him. "No. *Rex.* The douchebag I was dating."

"Now he's a douchebag?"

Trying to be calm, she answered. "Yeah. He broke up with me because I wear too much red." Conor burst into laughter. "It's not funny!"

"It's not funny that he broke up with you...but it's hilarious that he gave you a stupid reason like that."

"It's *not* funny." While she stared Conor down, she felt the corners of her lips twitching while she plopped back in one of the chairs in front of his desk. "Okay...it *is* funny. But that doesn't make him any less a shithead."

"Agreed. So…you wear too much red. Compared to who?"

"*Whom.* It's *compared to whom.*"

Shaking his head and giving his computer screen more attention again, he said, "I'm beginning to understand the troubles in your relationship."

"Thanks for cheering me up. Now I'll need a double therapy session. But enough about me. What did you need me for?"

"My question can wait till you're in a better frame of mind. Are you going to be okay? Do you need to go home early?"

Morgan smiled as she ran her hand over the polished surface of his desk, wiping off a few specks of dust, marveling how sweet Conor could be—when he wanted to be. "I'll live. Rex was an asshole anyway and, I guess, better to find out now instead of later, right? When I really started to fall for him?"

"That's a good way of looking at it. Relationships are—"

She interrupted him, quoting him. "—overrated. Yeah, I think I've heard that before. *You* might be happy being loveless for your entire miserable life, married to your business, but the rest of us want to spend our life with someone. Now…I can tell you I want to be with someone smart and funny and *nice*, not a douchebag like Rex, but I would like to find a good guy."

"Good luck with that."

"Maybe I'm just a poor judge of character."

"Maybe."

"Or maybe I'm just a magnet for shitty guys."

"Or maybe," Conor said, his full lips turned up in a smile, "all the good guys have been taken."

Morgan frowned. "Thanks, Conor. I always feel better talking to you." As he started smiling, she flipped him off.

He howled with laughter again. "I don't want to charge you for this session, so now it's time for you to listen to *my* problem."

"Oh, yeah. Just throw it in my face that you're actually employing me to work for you. Does this part fall under the *other duties as assigned* heading in my job description?"

Ignoring her remark, he said, "Here's the deal." Conor then stood up and walked across the room to glance out the window of his office over the buildings of the city toward the ocean. Morgan watched him, wondering what he was going to throw at her now—because he always had something brewing in that brilliant brain of his. "I was asking you about your high school reunion, because

5

I'm planning to go to mine."

"Why?"

"Never mind why. It's too long a story. But it's something I need to do. The problem is, if it's anything like my ten-year, I need to protect myself."

It was Morgan's turn to laugh. "Protect yourself? From what?"

"Again, another long story. Maybe I'll tell you on the flight there."

"What do you mean?"

He turned around and leaned his butt on the window sill. "I want to make you an offer, but you'd have to come with me." Morgan had a million questions but realized this wouldn't be an assignment she'd have to take notes for, so she waited patiently. "I need to appear, uh...unavailable. For multiple reasons. And the easiest way I can think of is to have a friend—an assistant—help me out."

She was feeling skeptical. "How?"

"Let me just say I'll make it worth your while, doubling your salary for one weekend." He smiled and pressed his fingertips together as if coming up with an incredible scheme. "I need you to work on your acting lessons...because, for one weekend only, I'm going to need you to play my wife."

CHAPTER TWO

THE LOVELY PEAL of Morgan's laughter filled Conor's small office. He'd chosen this space several years ago not just for the reasonable rent downtown but also for its ambience. The raw brick on one wall combined with the big windows on the other—not to mention great views of the city from their spot on the sixteenth floor of the building—made for a modern space that felt like a home away from home.

At a time like this, when the woman (the one person he spent more hours with than any other being on the planet) laughed raucously, he appreciated the acoustics in here. The sounds of Morgan's delight filled the room, reminding him that he didn't want any other space for his office.

Except for the fact that she seemed to be laughing *too much*.

As in…she thought it was amusing that he'd even bring up a fake marriage but there was no use talking about it more.

But he had to—because there'd be no selling her on the idea if she shut him down.

"That's rich, Conor." Morgan began to sit up, tossing her long dark brown hair behind her shoulders.

"No, I'm serious. Give me a minute to explain."

The thing Conor had always loved about Morgan was her willingness to do some of the silly tasks he requested, but this one most definitely took the cake. Actually, there was another thing he loved about the girl, and he hoped that was what would allow her to say *yes* to the strangest proposal he'd ever made to her (and the

7

funniness of the fact that he'd all but *literally* proposed to her was not lost on him). The willingness to go against the grain was due to Morgan's unorthodox nature, the part of her that loved to be a rebel, to upset the establishment. All he could hope for would be her inclination to upset the apple cart with him. "Did I ever tell you I was a total nerd in school?"

Morgan rolled her eyes, shifting in her seat. "Only a million times. It's a boring story."

"*Boring?*"

"Yes. Sorry, but I can't buy you as a bullied underdog, undervalued and unappreciated."

"And, yet, it's true." He saw a glimmer in her eyes as he spoke. What did that mean exactly? He had no time to worry about it, though; instead, he had some convincing to do. "And your disbelief doesn't change the past. Anyway…at my ten-year reunion, I'd hoped to reconnect with some of my gaming buddies, a lot of guys I hadn't kept in close touch with over the years. Facebook has never replaced real live human connection. But instead of reconnecting with old buddies, there were girls there ogling me, falling all over me, throwing themselves at me—the same girls who, ten years earlier, hadn't given a shit about who I was, what I did, or even what my name was. Now I'll admit it was a little fun—and funny—at first, but it got old fast. And at the twenty-year reunion, I want to talk to the real people, not the pretty people who want to rewrite history."

"And how exactly would *I* fit in…playing your wife?"

"Holy shit, Morgan. You don't have to say it as if it was the most disgusting thing I'd ever said to you."

Conor's insecurities about his looks had disappeared eons ago. For one thing, he realized the reality, which was that, even though he used to wear glasses and talked about so-called nerdy topics, he wasn't ugly—not by a long shot. And after his first year earning six digits, he invested in Lasik surgery and a personal trainer. Plus, on the advice of said trainer, he'd started wearing his hair in a messy bedhead look.

After his first year grossing over a million dollars, he no longer cared. And, since then, he hadn't had a hard time picking up a woman. While he knew the Lamborghini had a little to do with it, that wasn't all of it. He knew it was his confidence that won them over.

Still…until this very moment, he wouldn't have dreamed a tiny little pinch of insecurity continued to exist deep down. It was probably something he'd never be completely rid of—but he wouldn't admit that crap out loud and he would keep it buried forever.

Morgan put his mind mostly at ease. "Did I say it like that?" He shrugged, determined to not make a big deal out of it.

So…his wife. Yes, Morgan could pull it off. She was a few years younger than he, but he knew she could hold her own with the best of them. She had a snarky quality that made her seem like she was wise beyond her years. It was probably his favorite part about her.

Yes, her mouth—and the brain fueling it.

While she turned the idea over in her mind, Conor decided to as well. He wondered how well the two of them would be able to play husband and wife—and he had a niggling doubt that neither of them would be able to pull it off. He suspected the truly hitched folks at his reunion would smell their ruse a mile away.

Oh, and then there was the other problem…what if he really *did* find someone at the reunion he'd want to spend more time with? Then he'd look like a cheater—and that wouldn't go over well at all.

"Actually, let's not do the married couple thing—why don't you play my fiancée instead?"

"You're serious about this."

"Dead serious."

Morgan's green eyes flared so much that, had she been the sun, Conor's nose would have been singed. "You couldn't pay me enough to participate in something as fucking stupid as that." And she stormed out of his office.

If nothing else, her reaction made him laugh. "Was it something I said?"

Her last words echoed in his head. *You couldn't pay me enough.* Oh, yes, he could. He most certainly could. He just had to figure out her price.

As she did most mornings, Morgan woke up, turned on the coffee pot, and then grabbed the tiny notebook on which she had her personal daily to do list. Yes, she knew most of what was on it because she'd written it the day before, but she always felt accomplished when she was able to mark things off it. She took a deep breath as she flipped the cover.

Run around the block six times.

Half hour yoga.

Laundry.

Easy enough. Inspired by Conor, she'd been working up to running a mile every morning and six blocks was pretty close. Yesterday, she'd run for five blocks and alternated between walking and jogging for the last two—but today she was going for the whole distance. The yoga could come tonight after work when she usually appreciated it more, and laundry would also wait till then, considering she'd have to go to the basement and pray there was at least one empty machine in the building.

Her running suit was already on, so she grabbed the lanyard with her apartment key hanging beside the door and took the stairs to begin getting her heart rate up before her run. A little over ten minutes later, she was walking back up the stairs, catching her breath, and then walking in her door, enjoying the smell of coffee filling her kitchen. But a quick shower was in order first.

Morgan was congratulating herself on completing the entire mile. Tomorrow, she'd run the whole distance.

Wearing her fluffy pink robe and slippers, a white terrycloth towel wrapped around her head, she padded to the kitchen to reward herself with the first cup of coffee of the morning. It was also time to sit at the computer. Once she'd read the headlines of the day, she allowed herself to surf the internet—never more than half an hour—and she wound up on Facebook. And that reminded her…she still needed to change her status back to *single*. And it was in so doing that she noticed Rex was already in another relationship.

For reals?

For fucking *real???*

Morgan could feel her blood boiling, but her curiosity got the best of her. Rex hadn't unfriended her, so she allowed herself a peek at his profile. The new girlfriend looked a lot like her—long dark hair, thin eyebrows, almond eyes. Morgan felt anger at the other woman for a moment but then realized her ire was directed at the wrong person. That woman—Sandra, according to her profile—likely didn't know Rex was previously involved just hours earlier. Morgan was upset that she hadn't thought to check Facebook yesterday—before he'd broken up with her. If she had to guess, he'd changed his status right after lunch yesterday.

What a fucking asshole.

Yeah, she'd never planned on marrying the guy, but he couldn't wait a few days? God, she didn't even want to know what the hell he'd been thinking. She wasn't really that upset over Rex, the person; instead, she was irritated by Rex, the type. He'd been the last in a long string of shitty guys. How the hell did she manage to keep picking losers?

Shutting down her computer, she grabbed another cup of coffee and fumed the entire time she got herself ready for work. By the time she was walking out the door, she couldn't even remember styling her hair, putting on her makeup, or getting dressed. She looked down to see what clothes she had on: blue button-down shirt, black slacks, low black heels. Good enough.

Conor was busy writing a report when he heard Morgan unlock the front door of the office before entering. Her heels clicked on the tile floor as he imagined her walking to her desk and putting her things away. Not a minute had passed when she raised her voice to make sure he could hear her. "It doesn't matter how early I get here; you always beat me."

A moment later, she appeared in the doorway. "I'm the owner. Don't you think I should?"

"Yeah, I guess." She walked across the room and sat. "You know that weird, uh…request you asked me yesterday?"

Resisting the urge to smile, Conor nodded. The curiosity tickled his brain, but he had no intention of asking why she brought it up. "Yep." He removed his hands from the keyboard, sensing that Morgan wanted to talk now—and he was quite interested in what she had to say.

But he hadn't expected her response.

"I'll do it."

This seemed too good to be true. "Yeah?"

"Yeah—but only on one condition."

Was he going to regret this? He inhaled before saying, "Name it."

Her jade eyes lit up, and he couldn't tell exactly what that meant—but he knew he'd find out soon enough. "We make it convincing—mainly by changing our Facebook statuses to *engaged*."

That was an odd request—and it was one that could lead to huge problems. His current friends, for instance, would ask what the hell he'd been doing and why he hadn't told them before announcing it online—and his parents (well, his mother, anyway) would ask the same question and might take it personally that he hadn't said anything about having a girlfriend before. "Seems a little sudden, doesn't it?"

She cocked an eyebrow. "You started it."

Indeed. The feisty devil. While that was something Conor loved about her, it oftentimes worked against him. Still…she was actually considering helping him out, so he needed to see if he could make this work somehow. He squinted his left eye, something he did when he was negotiating. "Why not *in a relationship*? Or maybe *it's complicated*?"

He could tell by the glint in her eyes that she was mulling it over, but based on past behaviors, he expected her to put him through a little back and forth. Instead, she took a deep breath and said, "Fine. Okay. *In a relationship* it is."

Conor stuck out his hand and they shook on it. But he needed to know. "Why the change of heart?"

"I'll tell you *after* you tell me the perks."

He couldn't contain the laughter. "Of being my fiancée or just playing her?" Morgan folded her arms across her chest. "Well, like I said, I'll pay you overtime the entire time. You'll also get a free mini-vacation to colorful Colorado, and, uh…" He was going to make this shit up on the fly until he could tell she was completely sold. "Your wardrobe for the weekend. Food and lodging paid for, of course, and—spending money?"

Her lips curled up, but Conor wouldn't exactly describe it as a *smile*. "How much?"

"I don't know. A few hundred?"

"And where exactly are we going?"

"My hometown. Winchester, Colorado."

"And *that's* supposed to be a vacation?" Conor frowned until she grinned. "Should we shake on it again?"

"Have I ever screwed you over?"

"Fair enough."

"So…the answer."

"Rex and I just broke up yesterday and the stupid asshole is already in a relationship with another girl—so I need to let him know I can do the same damn thing."

Oh, poor kid. Conor hadn't understood yesterday how much the breakup had upset her—but she'd always put on a brave face, so it wasn't surprising. Suddenly, becoming engaged seemed even more drastic—but understandable. "Then…maybe I can help."

CHAPTER THREE

HOLY SHIT. MORGAN had always considered Conor a good boss and a decent friend, but she hadn't expected him to be quite this cool. Her story must have tugged on his heartstrings—if he had any. But she hadn't questioned it at the time.

Conor's helpful idea had been for the two of them to change their Facebook statuses to *engaged* at the same time. In the heat of the moment, that had seemed like a brilliant idea. Now, though, with her mother pestering her on the phone—thanks to her little sister freaking out about the Facebook announcement—she was questioning how smart that move had been. Of course, had she been paying attention to her phone to see the frantic text messages, she might have been able to prevent her mom's phone call. Instead, Dee hadn't been able to reach Morgan and had talked to their mother before Morgan had been able to text Dee back to explain what was happening.

It just reminded her why people still said *a stitch in time saves nine.*

"That doesn't make sense, Morgan. Even though you publicly announced it, you're just *pretending* to be engaged?"

"Yes, ma. My boss needs someone to play his fiancée at his high school reunion so all his old girlfriends or whatever don't cozy up to him just 'cause he has money now."

"And you had to do it on Facebook?"

"I don't expect you to understand."

"That's why I quit Facebook. People use it to air all their dirty

14

laundry."

"This isn't dirty laundry, ma."

Her mother sighed before telling Morgan she loved her. Then they talked about more pleasant things, like how Morgan's dad kept stacking his dirty socks next to his recliner. "I refuse to pick them up anymore. He wants them washed? He knows where the hamper is." After a few seconds, she added, "Except the family room's starting to stink."

"Let me know when he gets the clue." Until then, Morgan was going to avoid going home. Still, her father was just shy of being perfect—so it made sense that he'd have to have just one flaw, right? When she'd chatted for half an hour, she told her mom she had to start packing for the trip and so she had to go.

That wasn't entirely true. She had to go shopping first.

She'd managed to get some of her spending money out of Conor before leaving work for the day. "I need to look classy and sexy, right?" He'd rolled his eyes…but gave her his credit card and told her not to overdo it.

She bought three sets of casual clothes and two semi-formal dresses, one white and the other black, because, even though she hadn't gone to her own reunion, she remembered the schedule of events she'd avoided. His might be totally different, but she wanted to be prepared just the same. Either way, she was going to have an infusion of designer brands into her closet, thanks to the boss.

And then she let herself remember an old dirty little secret.

At one time, she'd had a huge crush on Conor.

Huge.

But the guy was truly married to his work—and loved casual, no-strings-attached hook ups. She knew now, though, that if she was ever going to have a chance at making him notice she was a woman, it was now. And, with that in mind, she shopped for a little lingerie and sexy underwear—after all, it was for him, right? A couple pair of shoes, some Obsession, and a little extra makeup, and she thought she was all set.

She'd be the perfect girlfriend. Er, fiancée. She'd make his old friends and would-be girlfriends jealous—and she'd make Conor look at her like the woman she was. She knew she was awesome girlfriend material, no matter what stupid Rex thought. She only had to convince Conor that real life relationships were more fun—and what she bought should do it. She'd have him eating out of the palm of her hand before he ever saw the credit card bill...

As the attendant took a ruler to Morgan's luggage, Conor turned his head and whispered, "You know we're flying back Sunday night, right?"

Her smile looked innocent, but he knew her better than that. "I've gotta look good, right?"

"Do I even want to know how much you spent?"

"Nope. You really don't."

"That's what I was afraid of."

"Ma'am," the man measuring the bag stood, "you're not going to be able to carry this luggage on."

"That's fine," Conor said. "We'll pay."

Unfortunately, Morgan was going to prove to be as stubborn with this guy as she usually was with Conor. "Look, it'll fit. I know it will. I just might have to squish it a little bit."

"I'm sorry, but that's not acceptable."

"If the effing TSA people hadn't needed me to take all my carefully packed stuff out and then—"

"I'm sorry, ma'am."

Though he was thankful that she was suppressing her potty mouth, Conor was starting to feel the back of his neck grow hot because he knew the people behind them were getting impatient—and he knew Morgan would be pissed because the man had called her *ma'am*. He wasn't sure which was worse—the crowd or his feisty employee.

"I can take some of it out and put it in my purse."

"I'll pay for it. Go ahead and take it." Morgan started to argue again but he lifted an eyebrow. That usually worked.

Fortunately, it did this time, too. She pinched her lips together as if a secret was trying to leap out. "Okay, sir. Thank you."

As the attendant waved them through, Morgan hissed, "I could have made it work."

"I'll take it out of your bonus." Keeping his eyes forward and hustling toward their seats, he made sure to avoid her face. Soon enough, though, he'd have to make eye contact. "Do you want the window or the aisle?"

"I don't care." Her tone was snippy—and that was okay, so long as she remembered who was boss.

Honestly, though, she was doing him a huge favor and he should be kissing her feet. "Then I'll take the window."

"Fine."

They sat in silence once they'd finagled their way in while others trickled down the aisle. Morgan absorbed herself in her phone, scrolling her Facebook feed. He looked out the window, grateful for a little downtime. Once the plane began taxiing down the runway, he whispered, "Do you want a drink?"

Her eyebrow arched, she asked without looking up from her phone. "You buying?"

It was the only thing that would make the flight bearable. "Yeah, so get ready to drink up."

With Morgan giggly, smiling, and undemanding—tipsy but not quite drunk—Conor noted that their flight was actually more than bearable. The time had seemed to, well, fly. And she wasn't stumbling drunk as they stood waiting for her bag to appear on the carousel.

As they walked through the airport and found a shuttle to take them to get their car rental, Morgan seemed to sober up—but Conor made a note to himself that if he needed her to chill just a little in the future, he would suggest a cocktail. But he didn't know how loose her lips would get with alcohol—and he felt like that was something he should know. She'd been his employee how long and he didn't know that about her?

Soon, they were zipping down the asphalt in a shiny black SUV—and that was when Morgan started talking, sounding as sober as ever.

"Dude…if you wanted to impress your classmates, you should've rented a Mercedes or a Corvette or something." Leaning forward, she turned the radio on and started scanning for a channel. He got ready to tell her he didn't feel the need to impress them but he didn't have a chance to speak. "How far?"

"Till we get there?" She nodded. "A little over an hour, give or take."

She frowned and leaned back after stopping on a station playing hip hop. Conor didn't know what her mood was all about but he had traffic to contend with—and the drive up the mountain should help her relax. If not, it didn't matter. He was paying her enough that she could pretend she was having the time of her life.

At first, Morgan had thought Colorado Springs, the city they were driving through, was where they were going to be spending the weekend but after twenty minutes or so, they were out of town, driving through the mountains. There was a house here and there and plenty of cars driving both ways, but they were most definitely leaving civilization.

Where the hell had Conor gone to high school anyway?

She adjusted the radio again, hoping it would keep her boss from talking. Her head was a little achy—nothing bad, but she figured it was due to a combination of one drink too many and the higher altitude. Why the hell had she allowed herself a couple of days ago to remember her one-time crush on Conor? What a stupid idea. They were friends—good friends, in fact—and the best way to maintain a friendly working relationship was to avoid having thoughts to the contrary. So she kept her eyes to the side of the road, looking at all the evergreen trees and other native vegetation and thought of the way Conor's actual girlfriend/ fiancée might act. Would she be girlie and prissy, expecting him to hold the door for her, fetch things, bring her flowers, and wait on her hand and foot or would she instead be a tough-as-nails businesswoman, fierce and formidable?

Aw, hell, who was Morgan kidding? She was no actress and, even if she were, she wouldn't be able to maintain a ruse like that for two days straight. Opinionated and mouthy, five minutes and all bets would be off—especially if Conor did one of those things where he got under her skin like he liked to do. No, it was better to just be herself and, if she didn't match people's expectations, there was no reason to worry about it. Again, it just a long weekend. She only had to pretend like she was in love with him for a couple of days.

A little while longer and Morgan began to see signs of

civilization again. There were two small car dealerships and a shopping center before they hit the first stoplight. Conor said, "I think it's too early to check into the hotel, but I thought I might go visit my folks if they're home. Do you want to come with?"

She figured they were nice enough people, but she didn't know if Conor had told them he was engaged to her or if it was just a joke. Either way, she imagined it might put her in an uncomfortable position, one her headache didn't want her to attempt. "Actually, if you wouldn't mind, I think I need an iced tea and maybe some soup or French fries or something."

"One too many mojitos on the plane?"

"Something like that."

"I can drop you off on Main Street. There are a lot of shops, touristy and otherwise, plus a few restaurants. When I leave my parents' house, I'll call or text you and pick you up wherever you are. Sound good?"

"Yeah." Except his town was looking pretty *dullsville*.

"If you need me to get you before that, just call."

"Fair enough." She picked her purse up off the floor of the vehicle and double checked that her phone and wallet were inside—because, you know, the alcohol.

Conor turned off the highway and drove up one block before turning again and said, "This is Main Street."

There was nothing spectacular about it, not that she'd expected anything mind-blowing. She imagined she was in the heart of small town Colorado, that a good many Main Streets in this state looked like this one, but she thrived in the big city. She couldn't imagine living in a tiny place like this. There was only one lane going each way in this downtown area, and she could probably even get away with jaywalking—without endangering her life. Looking at the cars parked along the curb at an angle (as well as noticing a few empty spots here and there) and observing that the tallest building here was three stories tops told her all she needed to know. She'd never say anything to Conor, but she was thoroughly underwhelmed.

"Have fun," she said as he drove off in the rental car. She made her way to the sidewalk and relished the feel of the sun on her shoulders. She'd walked only half a block when she realized she could smell flowers in the air, not an aroma she was used to in her neighborhood. Two blocks later, she was struck by the smell of fresh baking bread. Suddenly, she was ravenous—and calm.

In spite of the few cute shops along the way that caught her eye, she was now on a mission. At the end of the block, she spotted a place called Betty's Bakery and hoped that was the place whose bread she was smelling.

Assaulted by the hints of yeast in the air as she opened the door, she knew this had to be the place. But it didn't appear to just be a bakery. As she looked around, she noted that it was a full-blown restaurant. Maybe she *could* get a drink and snack here after all.

A woman behind the counter said, "Sit wherever you like, honey. I'll be right with you." Glancing around, she saw that she was the only customer. Maybe this place wasn't such a great idea after all—or maybe it was just because it was closing in on three, long before the dinner rush.

The woman walked out from behind the counter a minute later holding a glass of ice water and a menu covered in plastic. Morgan had chosen to sit in a booth at the window facing the street, wanting to people watch. If she got bored, she could always Facebook on her phone. When the waitress reached her, Morgan said, "Actually, I know what I want. I'd love a glass of iced tea, and the bread you're baking smells amazing."

"Those are rolls for dinner tonight, but I don't see why I couldn't give you one now. They'll be ready in a few minutes."

Five minutes later, Morgan was slathering butter all over a warm roll (one of two) and enjoying a cool drink. Two guys walked in and up to the counter.

Let the people watching begin.

Both men looked like they were businessmen beginning their weekend a few hours early—and, since they were stopping in here, she figured they had to be locals. They had nice shoes and slacks, long sleeved shirts and ties, but no jackets—telling her they must have offices somewhere nearby. As she watched them order drinks at the counter, she wondered if they were lawyers or insurance agents. Bankers, maybe? What other kinds of guys would have to wear suits in a small town like this?

Used car salesmen?

One of the guys—the one with slicked back dark hair and dimples to die for—turned and caught Morgan looking at him. He smiled, thankful he didn't seem to be offended, and she grinned back just as she heard a text notification ping on her phone. She glanced down and saw that it was Conor. If he was ready to pick her up, he hadn't visited with his folks for long. *Where are you?*

Betty's Bakery.

Nice. Be right there.

Glancing at the time on her phone, she saw that it was after three, so maybe Conor wanted to check in to the hotel now. Up until the time those interesting men had entered the bakery, she would have even considered going to his parents' house to meet them, because she wasn't exactly impressed with his old hometown. Now, though, she was enjoying the scenery. These men looked to be about Conor's age and not bad looking.

But there would be no scamming for guys here. That didn't mean she couldn't flirt, though. Both men had beers in their hands as they turned. Morgan hadn't even realized they served beer here—not that she would have taken it. Her headache was finally easing up from the alcohol she'd had on the plane. She needed to stay sober now.

After a minute chatting amongst themselves, the men made a beeline for her booth and asked, "Anyone sitting here?"

Morgan felt a smirk move her lips and she answered, "Yeah, the invisible man—and he won't stop eating my rolls."

The second guy, a cutie with spiky blond hair, said, "Want me to get you another?"

"I don't want to wind up *looking* like those rolls…so thank you, but no."

The first man, the one with black hair and dark brown eyes, asked, "So it's okay if we join you?"

"Why not? It's a free country."

The guy with black hair smiled and sat down, but he seemed reluctant to do so after acting eager moments earlier. The blond slid in the booth next to him and said, "Are you always so curt?"

"*Curt?* Hmm…I've never been called that. I've been called *snarky, bitchy, short, snappy, plucky, funny,* and even *rude* a time or two, but I've never been called *curt.*" After a moment, Morgan put down her phone to give them her full attention. "Maybe it's 'cause I'm a girl."

The guy with black hair smiled but the blond actually spoke. "Ah, clever."

"Yeah…my looks might attract but my personality pushes

people away."

The dark-haired man had a confused look on his face, like he was sorry they'd sat there, but the blond seemed amused. Morgan had nothing better to do until Conor got there, but the exchange had no goal, really. Once she left Betty's Bakery, she'd never see these guys again. Still, it could get awkward sitting here with nothing to do but stare at two decent-looking guys who didn't seem to get her. So she said, "I'm kidding. It's my version of West Coast charm. You like?" Both men smiled and nodded politely, no doubt considering leaving as soon as they downed their beers. Eh…easy come, easy go. She liked flirting but she didn't see any way she could actually date someone during the reunion, especially while playing fiancée. "You from around here?"

Blondie chose to answer again. "Kind of. You?"

Kind of? What did that even mean? "No. I'm here with a friend. I'm actually a California native."

"Yeah? Whereabouts?"

It was then that she heard the bell tinkle as the front door opened. Her back was to it, but she could tell from the guys' faces that they knew the person walking in, but it was the black-haired guy who said, "Conor Hammond. How the hell have you been?"

It was only a split second, but she saw the dark shadow cross her boss' face when she turned around to look. Who the hell was she sitting with and should she have known Conor would not be amused?

CHAPTER FOUR

"WELL, IF IT isn't Bill Bullock and Francis Mills. How the hell have you guys been?"

Bill, the blond, said to Morgan, "Excuse us a moment." Then he stood and said, "Great, never better. What about you?"

"Kicking ass and taking names. I see you've met my fiancée."

Francis, the man with black hair, raised an eyebrow but it was Bill who said, "Ah, is *this* fair young lady your fiancée? How much did you have to pay her to say that, Hammond?"

God, if these sons of bitches only knew. But he wasn't about to divulge that to these two assholes. And as upset as he'd been to see Morgan chatting with them, he felt a little appeased when she said, "Are you kidding? Conor's the best man I've ever known. He didn't have to ask me twice." She slid out of the booth and stood on her tiptoes to kiss his cheek. Damn. He'd have to give her a raise for thinking on her feet. "I'm the luckiest girl on the planet." She looked back at Bullock and Mills. "So did you go to school with these guys, honey?"

"Actually, yeah, I did. So I guess you'll be seeing more of them tomorrow." He turned to make eye contact with his old nemeses again. "You guys living here nowadays?"

"No. Are you kidding? We're in Colorado Springs running a construction company."

Running a company? He'd never imagined these two amounting to much of anything, let alone running a company, because they'd never seemed to apply themselves…so he was dubious, tending instead to believe that they were into some kind of petty crime. But he wasn't going to let them know he doubted them—because, in the grand scheme of things, it didn't matter. He'd left all this shit behind twenty years ago.

Hadn't he?

They would be a distant memory in less than a week.

"Nice. Well, see you guys at the reunion." To Morgan, he asked, "Ready?"

"Yep." She picked up her glass and slurped the last of the iced tea through the straw before pulling some dollar bills out of her purse. "Can I trust you guys to leave these there?" Bill looked like he was going to say something when Morgan said, "Just messin' with ya."

Ah…she was good, better than he would have expected. She had no idea the beautiful way she was setting them up and knocking them down. It was just like high school—only reversed. He could've kissed her then—but that would have been creepy. It was weird enough putting his arm around her shoulders as they walked out to the rental car.

Once they were out on the sidewalk, he said, "Ready to check in?"

"Yeah. You didn't visit your parents for very long."

"Mom tends to be a little neurotic. Plus, since my sister was over there, the novelty wore off quickly." Once they got to the car, Conor said, "Thank you, by the way. In case you couldn't tell, I'm not a big Bill or Francis fan."

"I suspected as much."

Conor snapped in his seat belt. "I say, after the long day, we settle in and call some room service. Sound good?"

"*Room service?* Don't you want to take me out to a nice restaurant?"

Starting up the car, he looked behind him before he said, "No. I'm going to have to deal with way too many of these fools come tomorrow evening, so I don't want to accidentally run in to anyone else before that. And I'm going to have to go back to my parents' house tomorrow afternoon to get that over with. Besides, you might not know it, but the hotel where we're staying is the finest dining you'll get in this burg."

The look on her face as he began driving forward told him she didn't believe him—but he didn't care. Once she saw the menu, she'd figure it out soon enough.

Less than fifteen minutes later, Conor was handing a few bills to the bellhop who'd brought their luggage up to the suite. First, Morgan gasped at how opulent the place looked and then, as she ran across the room and opened the door to the balcony, she marveled at the view. The Sedgwick had some of the best views of the mountains, but the ultimate sights were from its top floors—which was why Conor had sprung extra for the room he'd reserved earlier in the week. Honestly, that close to the reunion, he was lucky there were any free rooms at all.

It didn't hurt that all the cheaper rooms had already been booked—thanks to the reunion, no doubt. But Morgan didn't need to know that.

Closing the door, Conor turned to face Morgan—usually snarky, witty, quick, and sophisticated—and she looked at him, wide-eyed, her voice filled with an innocent quality that stirred up a strange feeling in his belly. "This place is amazing."

"I knew you'd like it."

She zipped off again in the other direction to check out the rest of their digs. As Conor searched the place for a USB port so he could charge his phone, she darted back in the main room with her face looking half-surprised, half-irritated. "There's only one bedroom, Conor."

"Oh, yeah, that. Appearances, Morgan. I doubt anyone from the reunion will be up here, but you never know. One bed looks like an engaged couple. Two don't. But don't worry—I plan to sleep on the couch."

"Are you sure?"

"Yeah. I want you to enjoy the full experience."

Grinning, Morgan darted back into the bedroom but seconds later, when Conor had finally located a port on the phone in the living area, she rushed in and grabbed her overstuffed suitcase. "I'm going to unpack."

Conor wouldn't have minded just living out of his luggage, but he needed to hang up a couple of things. As for the formal thing the reunion committee had going on tomorrow night, he'd get his old tux out of his old bedroom closet at his parents' house. He thought the whole formal-wear thing was silly, but if he was in for a penny, he was in for a pound. Fortunately, Morgan told him she'd already prepared.

He walked toward the bedroom, checking out the place along the way. He could see why Morgan had been a little excited. She came from a middle-class background just like he did, so a place like this was a little ritzier than they would have been used to growing up. Nowadays, though, he was a little jaded and couldn't get excited about something as superficial this.

The door was open, but he rapped on it to get her attention. "Mind if I grab a few hangers? I'll still need to borrow part of the closet."

"Yeah, go ahead." Morgan already had her suitcase open and an ironing board set up, the iron heating patiently. While she waited, she was busy putting items in drawers or the closet—or setting aside items to take to the bathroom later.

When Conor got to the closet, he saw no less than seven pairs of shoes on the floor. "Do we have a shoe addiction?"

Morgan glanced over at him from the dresser. "I'm a woman. Of course, I have a thing for shoes."

"And what's with all the red in here? I think I'm beginning—"

"Don't you even say it," Morgan said, glaring, picking up a red sneaker and threatening to whack him in the head with it.

Teasing, he said, "Sensitive," and left the room. He fished out the shirts and slacks he'd rolled up in the luggage, ones designed to need less pressing than others. As he took one of the shirts out, he noticed a few wrinkles, so he knew he'd have to do a little ironing before wearing it. Maybe when Morgan finished with hers. Lost in thought, he tossed them on the sofa but the big binder with information about local attractions and restaurants on the desk caught his eye. It was a little surreal staying in a hotel in his hometown, viewing it as an outsider, and he started wondering why he hadn't just stayed at his mom and dad's house.

Mom was neurotic. That was why. And probably *too* worried that he didn't have a *real* fiancée.

Flipping through the pages of the binder, he was reminded of some awesome places to eat, and the memories flooded his mind. There was no sense denying Morgan a little bit of fun because, beginning tomorrow night, she was going to be on the clock nonstop. If it was still in business, there was a really nice steak and seafood place just a few blocks from the hotel. Or they could eat at the restaurant in the hotel like he'd suggested before, but he considered leaving it up to Morgan after all.

He walked back in her room to hang up his clothes and said, "I hope you didn't eat too many rolls at Betty's Bakery."

"Why?"

"I'll take you out to eat."

Even though her eyes lit up, she said, "That's okay, Conor. I know you didn't want to go out."

"Nah. I want to. Just be ready in ten minutes."

"Really?"

"Yeah." He wasn't wearing anything spectacular but, really, he didn't need to. There'd never been an expected dress code at that restaurant, aside from the *no shirt, no shoes* rule. So he wandered around their suite, noting all the things they wouldn't be using: the little kitchenette, the big screen TV, and the fireplace (wrong time of year)—although, if they used the pool or the hot tub downstairs, they might decide a fire would be nice. He was flipping through the little HBO guide, considering switching the television on while he waited, until he heard her say, "Ready."

Conor was a little shocked. Morgan tended to dress in either office casual or pantsuits when they had a high-profile meeting. Now, though, she was wearing a black skirt that stopped above her knees and a red top that clung to her upper body enough that he was able to recognize her feminine features.

And tall *red* high heels.

Holy shit.

"You like?"

"Yeah. You look great." Maybe a little *too* great, because now Conor was forced to accept the fact that Morgan was a living, breathing woman. A *woman* and not just his assistant or friend.

He managed to keep any and all comments to himself until the valet driver brought the car back around. Once Conor was driving them out onto the street, he couldn't help himself and said, "By the way…those shoes make your legs look sexy."

*   *   *

Morgan hadn't blushed since her freshman year in high school—and the kids, friends and foe alike, had ridiculed her for how red her face had turned, and she'd vowed to never let the emotions of shame or embarrassment color her cheeks again. It was probably that moment that had transformed her into the Queen of Snark oh, so long ago. Not only had she taken up sarcasm like a coat of armor, but she'd also become artful at turning situations around. If a kid tried to embarrass her, she'd double down and lay it on thicker than anyone else ever could.

Of course, shortly after that, her classmates seemed to mature and back off, too...but it was too late. She'd grown to love and embrace that part of herself.

Now, though, she was looking out the passenger window seemingly at the street—while actually pondering Conor's words. Had he really said that—that her legs looked *sexy*?

And why the hell was she feeling a little excited by that?

She knew damn good and well why. When she'd started working for Conor several years ago, she'd first noticed his subtly handsome good looks. And then his demanding, sometimes assholish nature would anger and excite her at the same time. But it wasn't long before she realized he was married to his business and enjoyed playing a perpetual playboy. The occasional date seemed to be all he'd need to keep his single status in check. Morgan, realizing this and seeing that her low-key flirting didn't work (all while knowing that outright flirting could jeopardize her job), had finally given up and pursued other males—eventually, the crush disappeared. Problem solved.

Except it apparently hadn't.

But maybe she could push it back again. Once the weekend was over, she could return to business as usual, just like she had years ago.

"So, those guys back at the bakery."

"Yeah?"

"Enemies in high school, right? The only class we had together was Business Law, and it was clear to me back then that they were just jerking off. But then, ten years ago, they showed up at the reunion as owners of a new startup back east. They'd invented what they called an *environmentally friendly dishwasher*. It was portable, almost like a microwave, and you could install it under your counter or place it on a countertop. I swear to Christ, that's all those guys talked about—and all our classmates flocked around them like they were the best thing since sliced bread.

"When we all returned to our respective homes, they posted on Facebook that the company who bought their invention also chose not to produce it—supposedly. But it didn't matter. The popular guys stole the show. Jerking off, as usual. I'd been hoping to reconnect with the few friends I'd had and wound up getting to know a bunch of people I'd never hung with before. But the problem, I realized later, was that a lot of the women wanted to get cozy because I had money and my own business—and, unlike Bill and Francis, I was perceived as a nice guy. But it got even worse after the reunion. When everybody got home and started checking out my profile, they found out that I was no slouch—and then more people friended me and started messaging, wanting to ask if they were driving through California if they could swing by."

"That's why you're hardly on Facebook anymore?"

"Exactly."

And she wasn't going to ask, but she'd always gotten the feeling that Conor had been the ugly duckling in high school—one who'd bloomed into the beautiful swan she knew now. Actually, from what Conor had told her, it wasn't that he was ugly at all...but that he had no confidence. He'd *thought* he was undesirable and, in believing it, made it come true.

But he had transformed into the swan now—a hot, gorgeous swan, one that, once again, she was going to have a hard time getting over.

Why the hell had he said anything about her sexy legs?

CHAPTER FIVE

FRIDAY MORNING, MORGAN came out of the bedroom, feeling like shit. She'd never slept well in a hotel room, and this time was no different. The bedding was crisp and clean, the mattress firm yet comfortable, the pillows fluffy and comfy. The air in the bedroom was perfect, too—just on the cool side but not cold. And none of that mattered a bit because she was trying to snooze in a strange place.

But that wasn't all of it—she hadn't been able to stop thinking about Conor in the most inappropriate of ways. He was her boss and it didn't matter how hot he was, she had to get him off her mind.

He was sprawled out on the couch and the sheet he'd been covered with had slipped down enough that she could see his entire torso—lovely hairless pecs, tight abs…and a tattoo. A fucking tattoo! How come Conor had never told her about that?

At the risk of getting caught, Morgan tiptoed closer, hoping to get a look at it and maybe find out what it said—because, in the dim light of the room, she couldn't quite tell. As she neared the couch, though, she was able to see the ink was mostly words.

And that was when she ran into the coffee table.

"*Shit!*"

The actual noise of hitting the coffee table might not have awakened Conor, but her voice at the highest of decibels would.

"What? What the hell?" Conor bolted upright. Morgan knew that he'd figure out pretty quickly if she stayed in place that she'd gone out of her way to check him out, because the pathway between the door to her bedroom and anything else in the suite did *not* get close to the couch. Not even remotely. The couch was out of the way of everything else.

But she could come up with a quick explanation. "Sorry, Conor. I bumped into the coffee table and hurt my knee."

He was running a hand through his hair.

Damn, those biceps.

Morgan forced herself to walk it off, even though it hurt like hell, and she made her way toward the door. "Just checking to see if they left a paper in the hall like they said they would."

As she opened the front door and fetched said paper, she heard Conor say, "How long before you think you can be ready?"

The reunion shit didn't start till evening. "Ready for *what*?"

"A day on the town. Coffee first. Then I'm going to show you around, let you see some of the sights. Oh, and we have to get my tux at my parents' house." Morgan dropped the paper on the coffee table, hoping her face wouldn't betray just how un-fun all that sounded to her. "Since we're engaged, I thought the proper thing to do would be to meet my parents."

"Uh...they *do* know we're not *actually* engaged, right?"

Conor laughed. "Yes, of course. And I promise we won't be there forever but we're friends, and I know they'd like to meet you."

"Fair enough, but why didn't you just get your tux yesterday while you were there?"

"My sister was visiting, so I just sat on the porch with them talking. She hadn't seen me in a long time, and I thought it would be rude to make them follow my agenda. But there's only so much time I can spend with her so, after a while, I told them I needed to track you down and mentioned that I'd be back today."

"How convenient."

"We won't be there forever. Just long enough that, in the future, when I'm complaining about my pain-in-the-ass employee, they'll have a face to put with the name."

Flipping him off and making him laugh again, Morgan turned on her heel and began walking toward the bathroom. "Fine. Before we go, I need a while to shower and stuff."

"Wait a sec. I need to take a quick piss."

She turned on the light and stepped inside the door, peeking her face out. "Guess you shoulda thought of that *before* calling me a pain in the ass. Now I have a reputation to protect."

And, with that, she shut and locked the door before turning on the shower full blast and hopping in.

"Fucking A. This little vacation of yours has completely thrown me off my game."

"What do you mean?" Conor asked.

"I didn't write a to do list this morning—for probably the first time in three years."

Conor laughed, taking a sip of the cup of Americano he'd ordered at the small coffee shop. Both were also picking at cinnamon rolls, not the healthiest breakfast, but—as Morgan had noted—they were taking a break from the usual. Fortunately, he'd taken a jog on the treadmill in the exercise room while Morgan was showering, and he'd been able to find a restroom along the way. Maybe Morgan was off her game, but Conor was on his and hoped to be scoring points tonight.

He'd begun questioning why he wanted to go to this reunion anyway, because he'd already "proven" himself at the last one— and this time it was going to be a major pain since he and Morgan were playing the engagement game to keep the desperate women off him. Yeah, seeing his parents was always a plus, but he could take time off to visit them whenever he felt like it. But there was one reason why he really wanted to go. Aside from catching up with a few people he was interested in who weren't on Facebook much, he also wanted to visit with his buddy Steve Powell. The two of them had been in a gaming club together until the middle of their junior year. Steve and a girl in the club had gotten pretty serious with each other and, if Conor remembered correctly, she'd gotten pregnant and Steve, being an upstanding guy, had started working nights to help pay for the baby—but the two of them didn't actually get married until after Conor had left for college.

And Steve hadn't been at the last reunion, either, but Conor had messaged him on Facebook last Christmas and got a reply in February. Steve told him he'd be there. That was when Conor had started mulling it over in his mind, debating if he'd lost said mind as he recalled the last reunion and the clingy women who'd wanted to be his friend after ignoring him all those years.

"Penny for your thoughts, boss."

Conor shook his head, realizing he'd tuned out and saw that Morgan had a small notebook and pen beside her plate. "Sorry. I was just wondering how my friend Steve's been all these years. Haven't seen him since the summer before I left for college."

"You'll find out tonight." Morgan wiped her fingers on the white paper napkin. "So…to do list, Conor. What have we got to do today?"

"You already said this is like a vacation, Mo. That means you don't have to write a list."

No way would he tell her the scowl on her face made her look cute. "Fuck that. I don't feel right if I don't."

"Fine. Then how about this? Shower? Check. Breakfast? Check. Part of it's already done. Next, *get tux at Conor's parents' house, get ready for reunion, go to reunion.* That work?"

"I still don't get why you didn't just get your tux yesterday."

Conor cut a piece of cinnamon roll off with his fork. "Are you nervous about meeting my parents? Might I remind *you* we're not actually engaged?"

"Yeah, right. That's it. I'm nervous about meeting your parents."

"It's not like we have a lot to do this afternoon anyway. It won't take us hours to get ready." He sliced at the roll on the plate again. "Well, *you* maybe, but I just have to get dressed."

"You want me to look good or not? I could easily wear a pair of shitty sweats and rat out my hair. That would keep those crazy women at bay."

He couldn't help laughing again. "When you finish there, we'll walk up and down Main Street just so I can show you the town a little bit."

"I already knocked that off my list yesterday…but I guess we're going to repeat all that today, huh?"

"You didn't have a tour guide then."

Morgan arched an eyebrow—but then she penciled *exercise* onto her to do list before polishing off her cinnamon roll.

*   *   *

Morgan wouldn't admit it out loud to Conor, but she enjoyed seeing his hometown through his eyes. Being here gave him an enthusiastic, boyish spring in his step and a devilish twinkle in his brown eyes that she hadn't seen before.

It made him adorable and all but irresistible—so much so that Morgan laced her arm through his and, when he gave her a look of confusion, she said, "We actually look engaged this way, Conor."

Once they'd strolled the length of Main Street, they crossed the road and began walking down the other side. At the next block, Conor stopped. "Holy shit. This place is still here."

Morgan looked at the sign: *Games and Fortune.* Then she glanced in the windows. It looked like a used game store, but there were all sorts of paraphernalia inside, too—from the sidewalk, it looked like they had costumes, books, trinkets, and collector memorabilia.

"Geek's paradise," she muttered.

Conor must not have heard her because he said, "Oh, my God. Vince is in there."

"*Vince?*"

"Yeah, the owner."

"It *is* after ten, boss. He's got a business to run."

"Yeah, I guess so. And since school's out, it might pay to open early." Conor shook his head. "I wonder how old Vince is doing. He wasn't much older than my friends and I when he opened the place. I think I was a sophomore then. We'd bring our old games down and trade 'em in for ones we hadn't played. Or if a controller broke, he always had used ones in stock for cheap—not that they were worth the money. But Vince was a great guy just to talk to."

Conor's hand wrapped around the door handle before Morgan could even try to stop him.

Great.

Well, at least this visit would give Morgan plenty of fodder for ribbing Conor in the future. She never would have pegged him as a gaming guy. She wasn't positive, but she didn't think he played a lot of games nowadays—and he'd had no problem telling her he'd been a nerd as a kid, but she'd had no idea just how much of a nerd he'd been.

When they walked in, Vince, a balding guy in decent shape, had a game controller on the counter and a screwdriver in hand.

He looked up and gave them a quick greeting before returning to the task at hand. "Vince?" Conor asked, approaching the counter. The man looked up again. "Do you remember me?"

The man gave a half-hearted grin. "The reunion starts tonight, yeah? You know how many guys have been in here already askin' me that?"

"Fair enough. But I was one of your first customers—me and my buddies. I think you called us the *Nintendo Brats.*"

It was then that Vince scrutinized the man in front of him. "Yeah, I remember that."

"It was me and Steve Powell and Leo Lane—and a couple of other kids who hung with us off and on."

"So you must be...Conor Hammond?"

"I knew it. You *do* remember me!" Conor and Vince shook hands. "How's business been?"

"Not bad, but nothing like the glory days."

Morgan leaned in past Conor and stuck out her hand. "Hi. I'm Conor's fiancée, Morgan Tredway." Giving Conor an evil glare out of the corner of her eye, she said, "I know I can't compare to the likes of Zelda, Princess Peach, and Lara Croft, but I thought I'd introduce myself anyway."

Vince had a weird look on his face, as if he'd just sucked on a lemon. "Nice to meet you. Was that dig at me, Conor, or both of us?"

Morgan smiled, realizing she'd once again come off as a bitch. Normally, she wouldn't care, but she had a feeling from the way this guy had said it that he got more than his fair share of shit. "Sorry. Just my future husband. Seriously, Vince, what's a girl supposed to think when her boyfriend ignores her all the time?"

His eyes twinkled. "I'd think, with a gorgeous gal like yourself, that he's fixing to get an ass-whoopin'." Well...maybe *that* was a little extreme. "You *do* play, right?"

"Games?"

Now was Conor's turn to laugh. "You don't have to say it like you'll get a disease. No, she doesn't."

"You don't anymore, either, Conor." To Vince, she added, "He's a bit of a workaholic."

"It's hard not to be come tax time."

"What do you do nowadays?"

"Accounting. It's not what I set out to do...but it kind of

found me, you know? I started school majoring in applied math and minoring in computer science but, by my second year, I decided I was drawn to money. After I graduated, I found a job with a great accounting firm but I saw so many things that they did that I thought, 'If I had my own company, I'd do it *this* way.' After saying that over and over, I asked myself why the hell I wasn't doing it my own way. So, before I was thirty, I was opening my own business."

"It's hard to beat not having to report to a boss, don't you think?"

Morgan said, "You've never had *this* guy as a boss."

Vince tilted his head before picking up the screwdriver again. "You work for your boyfriend?"

"Yeah."

"I've heard that's a bad idea."

"You got that right," Conor said, and Morgan stuck her tongue out at him.

"Morgan, right?" She nodded at Vince. "I have a story for you—and you'll maybe understand that Conor here has always had the entrepreneurial spirit. So I opened this little game shop back then, because opening a business was a dream of mine, and even though I didn't have tons of items, I did have enough to make a go of it. Not only had I bought lots of used games and systems online, but I also hit garage sales and things like that. I'd been repairing my own consoles for years, so after running a short-lived online shop, mostly to gain more products, I rented a store front and voilà.

"But the store you see is not how it began.

"I only sold games and game systems—but when Conor here and a couple of his buddies swung in, they told me they'd love gaming mags and memorabilia and stuff along those lines, so I figured out how to get that stuff in there.

"But what changed everything was the day Conor asked if I'd host a tournament. At first, I thought, 'Why the hell would I want a bunch of kids in here, rowdy and making noise and getting into everything?' And then, after a day or so, I wondered what the hell my brain damage was. Kids were my target demographic. Sure, I had a couple of older people walk in the doors—and I still do today—but back then, it was mostly kids, especially ones in high school. So I organized an annual tournament and it's played right over there." He pointed to one of the front windows. "I clear out those t-shirt racks and move a big table over. A couple of months before, I survey the kids to see what hot new game is out there that could work for a tournament. Fighting games are best, but you never know. Sometimes we do large teams and two separate versions of the same game. But it draws a crowd and reminds people I'm here—free advertisement. Plus, during the tournament, I sell drinks and snacks, and between the event and the exposure afterward, I finish the year with a profit."

"That's thanks to *me*?" Conor asked.

"Yeah, man. Totally. If you hadn't asked, I don't know that I would have thought of it. So thanks again."

Conor shook his head. "Sure—but you're the guy who ran with it. You actually inspired *me*. I don't think I would have considered becoming a business owner if not for you."

"Ah…it's a regular love fest," Morgan said. She couldn't help her usual snarky nature, but the truth was this little story had put Conor in a completely new light. Maybe he really was a good guy through and through.

Conor ignored her. "It helped me put together a solid group of friends. We'd been half-hearted before, but once we started the tournament, we embraced our nerdiness."

"And yet, as I recall, you stopped coming to my shop *before* you graduated and left town—but your buddies kept coming."

A wry frown threatened to cover Conor's face. "That was stupid, but I'd thought maybe if I disavowed my nerdy nature, I'd have a better chance of getting a gorgeous date for prom."

"Can't blame you for that. Did it work?"

"Nope." Conor glanced at Morgan and winked before he said, "But money does."

As Conor pulled the rental car in front of the red-brick two story home of Edgar and Dale Hammond, his parents, he was questioning if this had been a good idea. His mom was fussy and neurotic nowadays, his dad half deaf and sometimes grouchy, and this whole thing could end with him feeling frustrated as hell. He might leave with his tux draped over his arm but with stress levels elevated, too—and he knew he had to be confident, suave, and cool as a cucumber tonight.

If shit gets tense, we just leave. Easy.

But there the four of them were, drinking iced tea and eating mom's homemade peanut butter cookies, having a good time laughing and joking.

At his expense…but still.

"It's true," his mom said. "Conor was practically naked all the time until he had to start kindergarten—and even then, once he got home, there went all the clothes." She mimicked tossing clothing off her arms like a dancer might flourish her limbs.

Morgan was laughing her ass off. Conor tried not to sound butt hurt, but he was tired of the stories. "Okay, so it's funny…but it's not *that* funny."

"Yes, it's a riot!" she practically squealed, her giggles ending in a snort.

Definitely not that funny.

Why had he thought it would be a great idea to bring Morgan to meet his parents?

"If it makes you feel better," Morgan said to his mom, "he keeps his clothes on at work all day long." Morgan turned her face to him and winked, patting him on the forearm.

Interesting. That felt almost…*affectionate.*

"Seriously, though, in case you hadn't already figured it out, I wanted to mention that your son is a genius and really good with people."

"Hard to ignore the genius part," his dad said. It was nice to know his parents were proud of him.

"Why did you want your old tuxedo, son?"

"I don't own another tux, mom, and it would be stupid to buy one just for the reunion."

"With you living in the big city, I'm surprised you haven't needed one by now." He wasn't going to tell his mother, but he'd rented one or two in the past—and he didn't want to make it a habit. He wasn't high profile enough that he had to wear them very often. And even if he did, there was no way he wanted to tote it around on a flight. "But what if it doesn't fit?"

"Why wouldn't it?"

His mom set her glass of iced tea down, a grin on her face. "When's the last time you wore it?" Conor racked his brain and felt a little discouraged when he figured it out. "Your senior year.

Honey, you've filled out a lot since then."

Morgan glanced at him, looking like she was stifling another laugh. "Maybe you should try it on now. If it doesn't fit, we could probably rent a tux somewhere."

She was right, but what a pain in the ass—and he didn't want to dress in one anyway. He was more of the dot-com variety of office casual. But when he had to dress like business, he had a few expensive suits to wear, ones he'd purchased and had tailored to impress. A tux seemed overly formal and he didn't plan to attend any red carpet events where he'd have to go overboard. In fact, this damned reunion was the first time in years he'd needed anything like that.

But both women were spot on. It had been a long time since he'd worn the old one. It wasn't out of style, but he wasn't a scrawny, nerdy teenager anymore.

Morgan followed him upstairs to his old bedroom. Well, honestly, it was no longer a bedroom. The closet was full of his stuff, but his mom had converted the rest of the room into a crafts den. She created all kinds of homey decorations all winter long (plus candles and soap) and then sold her creations at different fairs, bazaars, and flea markets all summer long. As Conor opened the door to the room full of fabrics, sequins, hot glue, and ribbons, assaulted by the scents of cinnamon and pomegranate, he realized that, perhaps, he'd gotten his entrepreneurial spirit from his mother.

"This is your old bedroom, Conor?" Morgan asked as they walked in. "Is there something you want to tell me?"

"You're quite the comedienne, but don't give up your day job." He opened up the door to the closet. It was crammed full of boxes and a few clothes, including his graduation gowns, hung from the rod. The tuxedo was pushed to the far left, and he pulled it out.

Morgan winced but said nothing. He eyeballed it, afraid they were right. He wasn't worried about the pants. He'd brought a pair of black dress slacks that would work if needed. "Just try the jacket on," Morgan said. "If it fits, then the shirt might, too." Was she reading his mind?

"Okay." He slipped the jacket off the hanger. "Here. Hold this." Then he started sliding his arm into one sleeve, and it was tight before he could get it all the way up to his shoulder.

Just then, his mother walked in. "Do you want me to alter it, honey? I've got my sewing machine right here."

If she were shrinking it down, that might be manageable, but there was no way he could see her making it bigger. "I don't think that's doable, mom. I think Morgan had the right idea. It's Friday afternoon—so I should be able to rent one. Is Wash and Go still in business? And do they still rent tuxedos?"

"They're still in business but I don't know."

Morgan already had her phone in hand. "Hold on," she said, swiping at the screen. "Looks like it, but just a sec." Then she put the phone to her ear.

She began talking into her cell while Conor's mother asked him, "Do you want me to donate it to a thrift store or would you rather I alter it for you to wear another time?"

"No, ma. If you want, you can get rid of it."

"You're six-four, right?"

Morgan's question threw him off guard momentarily. "Uh, yeah." How did she know that?

She started speaking in the phone again and his mother said, "You might want to go through the rest of those clothes."

Grinning, he said, "Maybe." There wasn't much and he knew it was stupid—but the rest of the clothes hanging in there had memories attached to them. The tux? That was easy to let go.

Then again, he'd moved past all that. He hadn't looked in there in a decade, so he obviously didn't need any of it.

"You can get rid of it if you want, mom. Then you'll have the closet all to yourself."

Morgan hung up. "They can hook you up, Conor, but we need to get you there now. They said they're almost out of your size."

Raising his eyebrows, he nodded. "Sorry, mom. Gotta go."

"I know. I'm glad you came again and brought your girlfriend this time."

"She's not my girlfriend."

As they walked out of the room, Morgan teased, her voice low enough that his mom couldn't hear, "Jesus H. You don't have to be so emphatic about it."

Did she feel insulted?

Halfway down the stairs, his mother said, "Those sequins are a pain in the butt to vacuum up when they fall into the carpet. I'm thinking about pulling the carpet out and putting in a wood floor, so I can sweep it up."

"Good idea."

Once downstairs, they headed outside with his dad in tow. Morgan hugged them both and said she was glad to meet them, and his dad said, "Thanks for keeping Conor's head on straight."

"Somebody's gotta do it. Nice to meet you both." She jumped in the rental car and started playing on her phone. Probably checking emails, if Conor guessed right.

"Come see us Sunday before you leave if you can, son."

"Will do, dad." After hugging his father, he embraced his mother and kissed her on the cheek.

"I like her, Conor."

Agreeing, he said, "She's great."

"Actually, I *love* her. I think she's a keeper, son. If nothing else, she's a heck of an assistant. Figured all that out before I could even pull out the phone book."

As Conor began driving down the road toward Wash and Go, a thought embraced his brain. *Mom had hated every last one of his girlfriends…and yet she loved Morgan, his fake girlfriend.* What did that even mean?

And why could he not stop thinking about her that way?

CHAPTER SIX

CONOR WAS ADJUSTING a bowtie inside the dressing room, but he could hear Morgan's voice just outside. "So why the hell did you have a tux if you never went to prom, Conor?"

"I didn't say I didn't go to prom."

"But—"

Opening the dressing room door, he stopped Morgan in her train of thought. "I took one of my gaming friends." Morgan squinted an eye at him. "A *girl* gaming friend."

She continued scrutinizing him, but she was now looking at the suit instead of his face—and she didn't appear impressed.

"Sir, I think that looks perfect," the tailor said as he walked over to join them, looking Conor over from head to toe.

"Fuckballs. Are you and I looking at the same guy?" Morgan interrupted. "Sorry, Conor, but your ugly high school tux would have looked better than this."

The tailor, an eyebrow arched, countered, "We don't have a big selection left."

"Bullshit. You have that rack right there. You said those weren't rented out."

"Yes, but they're the wrong size."

"Can't you adjust them?"

The man's nostrils flared, the only indication Conor had that the man was growing angry—but he wasn't going to say a word. He'd had these sort of skirmishes with Morgan before, and there was no winning them. Once she got it in her mind that she was right, only a miracle could alter her perception. "You said you needed the tux today."

"Ah, good, you understand basic English."

And how many times had he told her she'd get more with honey than with vinegar? "Morgan, why don't you let me handle this?" Moving over so the man turned in order to take Morgan out of his direct line of vision, Conor asked, "Do you have anything else maybe? I think I agree that this one isn't my style."

"As I said, sir, for your height, this is all we have left."

"What's wrong with these ones my assistant pointed out?"

"They'd all need alterations. Didn't you say you needed this tonight?"

"Technically, no. I need it by tomorrow night—but we're going to be busy all day tomorrow and possibly unable to get back here."

Conor could practically see the man making mental calculations in his brain but he didn't have a chance to counter before Morgan jumped in again. "What if we gave you five-hundred dollars to get it done in an hour?"

The man's caterpillar eyebrows gave away his shock but that quickly melted into slick subservience.

And what the hell was Morgan thinking? Just because he had money didn't mean he wanted to spend that much on alterations. He could have probably bought a tux for that price. The tailor walked over to the rack that, moments earlier, he'd said he couldn't rent to them, and Conor took the time to look at her with widened eyes, hoping he communicated the sense of incredulity he felt. She whispered, "Do you want to look like a goofy little shithead kid—or do you want to look like a successful businessman?"

She had a point—but, dammit, why did she always have to be right?

The man turned around, hanger in hand, and said, "This one would only need—"

"No, that one won't do."

Conor asked, "What's wrong with it?"

"Pinstripes. That's a hard nope. Next."

One thing Morgan had nailed on the head, though, was the man's willingness to work with them when money was on the table.

The man had barely touched another hanger when she said, "Absolutely not. The jacket and pants need to be solid black."

"I don't see—"

Morgan interrupted Conor as well. "Do you want to look good?"

"Of course."

"And like you didn't spend twenty-five dollars at a yard sale?" Conor could only let out a frustrated breath of air before she continued. "Then trust me." She walked over to the rack and pointed to a couple of them. Then she and the tailor began haggling back and forth, with only a few expletives from Morgan's mouth.

At that moment, he decided to let it go. Morgan was not only handling it, she seemed to be enjoying the process. Yes, it meant he was spending more than double what he'd planned for the rental, but this kind of bullshit was what he'd always paid her for. He took care of the numbers, making money by keeping his clients' financial affairs in order, and Morgan kept him organized and, for the most part, kept the clients happy, too.

She was worth her weight in gold—but he wouldn't say so, because that could easily go to her head.

"Yes, this one would be easy enough, I think, and I could have it done by closing."

Morgan, a large grin plastered on her face, held the tux up so Conor could see it. "What do you think?"

Before he could even shrug, the tailor said, "I'll need you to try it on first, sir."

In just a few minutes, Conor joined them outside the dressing room while the tailor fussed, taking measurements. Even though Conor had never sewed before, it didn't look like it would require too much. The man was talking about letting out the hem on the pants and arms, but Conor was only half listening. Instead, he was looking at Morgan. She kept a close eye on the tailor and asked a question or two, but it was clear that she had Conor's best interests at heart. What would he ever do without her?

He hoped he'd never find out.

Morgan had pulled the bottom of her skirt down, trying to make it ride lower. Sitting in the chair in their room, she'd thought it would look better when she stood, but damned if it wasn't a little

44

too snug and a little too short. It wasn't until they were standing in front of the elevator waiting for the doors to open when she asked, "Conor, if I promise to hurry, could we go back to our room so I can change really quick?"

"Why? It looks great."

"I look like a slut."

"No, you don't." He glanced at her knees before returning his eyes to the elevator.

"Yeah, I do. My fucking hem is just inches away from my ass. But the worst part is how my boobs stand out."

"Nah. The black fabric makes them less noticeable."

And what the hell was that even supposed to mean?

"Whatever. Just don't be surprised when a lot of your classmates hit on me."

She could have sworn she heard some guttural noise rumble in his throat, but even if not, she was certain she could sense it. Good. She wanted him jealous. It could lead to a few fun things between them.

To add a little more fuel to that fire, she added, "At least that'll give me something to do."

This time, Conor said, "Hmm," and left it at that.

"It'll also help solidify how serious you are about your business. I mean seriously. Even your fiancée can't keep your attention for long."

"You seem to be having a lot of fun with this."

"Shouldn't I be? I seem to remember my boss saying work doesn't feel hard when you enjoy yourself."

"Using my words against me. Typical."

Soon, they were riding the elevator to the ground floor. Morgan had been thinking this two-horse town with a population of about two-hundred was as backwoods as it could get, but this hotel could have easily fit into any of a number of gorgeous downtown urban settings.

Morgan paused, arched an eyebrow at Conor, and shook her head, but he dropped his phone in his jacket pocket, an eyebrow raised as if mirroring her face, and he held out his arm to lead her inside.

"You're gonna make me do this."

"I'm telling you you look *fantastic*, Morgan."

She wasn't going to argue it any longer. As they walked down the hall, Morgan couldn't keep her snarkiness contained any longer. "Obsequious much?"

"I gotta tell ya, Mo, that's one of the things I love about you."

"What?"

"Ya know big wurds," he said with a phony backwoods drawl.

She giggled. "You implying we're walking into a den of not-so-smart?"

"No, not at all. In fact, I'm looking forward to catching up with some of my old buddies."

"Well, that's good. Isn't that why we're here?"

He nodded but didn't look at her or say a word. Soon, they found the signs leading the way to the reunion, which was apparently being held in a ballroom. For some stupid reason, Morgan suddenly felt intimidated, something she hadn't felt since childhood.

A *ballroom*?

It was silly, though. Yes, she would have felt more comfortable in a business-type suit like Conor wore. Business *casual*. He wore the suit but no tie, and he looked relaxed but professional. She, on the other hand, looked like she was getting ready to hover on a street corner, waiting for a date.

But if anyone could pull it off, it was Morgan—and because she was a little younger than these folks and her clothes showed off her body, she was sending the signal that Conor needed her to—so she chose to chill out.

They walked up to a table just outside the large room, meant for registration. The beautiful brunette tilted her head and first examined Morgan's face before realizing she was probably too young to have graduated with them—either that, or she had a killer skincare routine. She assessed Conor next and said, "Don't tell me. Let me guess." She continued to scan his face. "Don't tell!" Then she picked up a bundle of papers and began reading them, flipping a page every few seconds. "You're not Brian Bush." Tapping her upper lip with her perfectly manicured russet fingernail, she put her nose back in the papers before she let out a squeal moments later. "Oh, my gosh! You're Conor Hammond!" Jumping up, the woman ran around the desk, arms spread wide for a hug.

Conor said, "Hello. How have you been?" but that wasn't enough for the girl.

"You don't remember me, do you?"

He examined her face once more and said, "You look kind of familiar but I'm sorry. You're right. I can't place your name." Giggling, she leaned over as if telling a secret. That she whispered helped. "I had a nose job three years ago. Best thing I ever did."

Morgan, tired of playing third wheel, said, "It looks great."

"Thank you so much. And you are...?"

"Morgan Tredway. Conor's fiancée."

"Ooh, fiancée, huh?" She giggled again, an obnoxious sound that was going to drive Morgan crazy if she had to be around it much longer. "I hope you don't find the stories about our high school days too boring." She didn't even give Morgan a chance to answer before she turned and started flipping through more sheets. "Here's your nametags." She handed Conor a nametag covered in plastic, attached to a lanyard, and then she handed another to Morgan. "Hang on to those, because they'll get you in to all our functions this weekend."

Morgan glanced down at hers. It had her first name only—below that, it had Conor's name in parentheses. She thought about making a smart-ass comment about being treated like a second-class citizen or some shit, but she understood. This wasn't *her* high school reunion, after all, and she didn't need a red-carpet welcome.

But the chatty woman wasn't done. She handed them both little red ticket stubs. "Cash bar tonight, but the first one's free. Just present this to the bartender and he'll hook you up."

Conor took a guess. "Cheerleader?"

"Oh, you are a sweet one. Thank you, but no. I was on the dance team and in choir."

"So are you going to leave me in the dark all night?"

Cackling, the woman pushed her hair back over her left shoulder before pulling her lanyard out from her jacket, revealing the nametag. "Kendra."

"Kendra. I think we had biology together."

"Yes, exactly. Anyway...the name was *Johnson* for a while, but my divorce was finalized last month, so I'm once again Kendra King."

"You look fantastic, Kendra."

"So do you, Conor."

Morgan was ready to puke. "Let's go hit the bar, babe." A fiancée would call him that, right?

Blinking as if breaking a spell, Conor looked down at Morgan, nodding. "Catch you around, Kendra."

The perky classmate tittered and then greeted another couple walking in the door. Morgan said, "Are they all like that?"

The smirk on his face made him look kissable, damn him. "You jealous?"

"Only because I'm your fiancée. I *should* be upset, shouldn't I?"

His laughter followed them through the doorway. "I love it when you're angry, so why not?"

Frowning, she got ready to come back with a curse-laden bite, but Conor was practically tackled by a balding guy with a pot belly and gray strands in the hair he had left. "Conor Hammond. How the hell are you?"

Conor smiled, allowing himself to be pulled into the embrace of the burly, jovial man. "Dave? Dave Shivers?"

"That's me. What you been up to, smart guy?"

"Same old, same old."

The man looked at Morgan. "I see he's humble as ever. Who's your date, Hammond?"

Morgan flashed a bright smile; this time, it came easily. "I'm Conor's fiancée, Morgan Tredway."

"Oh, my. He's a lucky man, Morgan. I can tell from your handshake that you're a little feisty. A man like Conor needs a woman like you to keep him on his toes."

"Ha. He needs a woman like me to keep his shit organized."

Dave turned his attention to Conor. "I love this gal already. I think she's a keeper."

"Thanks. I think so, too."

"Just me, though, or are you robbing the cradle a little bit?"

"He's not *that* much older than me."

"Besides, she's wise beyond her years."

Morgan laughed so hard she snorted. "That's just the smart ass in me."

The way Dave assessed them made Morgan certain the jig was up. If he figured out the engagement was just a ruse, Conor might hold that against her—not that she was up against anyone else for an Employee of the Year award. But Dave said, "If this guy doesn't treat you right, you come see ol' Uncle Dave. I know your boy here has lots of money, but I think I've got him beat in that department."

"Oh, really?" Jokingly, Morgan took his arm, pretending to cozy up next to him. She hoped it would distract him from the truth that she and her boss weren't really a couple.

"How many times have you been married, Dave?"

"Counting the divorce I'm going through now?"

"You made my point for me, you scoundrel. I think Kendra back there is looking for a new man."

"Yeah? Lemme at 'er."

Conor's eyebrows were raised once Dave walked away. "What am I gonna do with you, Morgan? You're here to make my life *easier.*"

"I tried to warn you, boss. I can't help it if all these old men think I'm hot."

"Oh, I'm an old man now?"

"If the shoe fits." Keeping her ire in check, she snatched the drink coupons out of Conor's hand and began marching toward the bar across the room. "You coming?"

She only hoped there was enough alcohol to make this fucking night bearable...

CHAPTER SEVEN

CONOR HELD IN his hand a Jack and Coke. While he hadn't given it too much thought, he'd considered what his drink would signal to his old classmates. A beer didn't seem too bad a choice, but it also lacked the air of sophistication he hoped to communicate. The drink he sipped told them all that he was manly and no nonsense.

At least, he hoped so.

Just like at his ten-year reunion, the women sniffed him out like a bloodhound might track a rabbit. He found it odd, because he knew some of his other classmates had become successful, and they were single and good looking.

Maybe the gold diggers scoped all those men out, hoping to find a winner.

First there was Amber. Morgan had excused herself, whispering in his ear first, and he got the feeling she just needed a breather. He'd been talking to a couple of male classmates when those guys decided they needed more beer—and, in that short second that he found himself alone, Amber approached him. "Well, well, well. If it isn't Conor Hammond. I swear you look even better than our last reunion."

"Hi, Amber." Maybe she was just being friendly, right? He didn't want to be rude, but he couldn't say the same thing about her. She didn't look bad, but she looked her age—and, based on past experience, he thought it best not to encourage her. "How have you been?"

She insisted on hugging him and she held on a little longer than she should have.

Was she sniffing his cologne?

"Oh, you know. My kids are in high school now. Well, not all of them. My youngest is in middle school. But I'm just plugging away."

This was okay. Nothing too strange, so he could continue being polite. "Where are you working?"

"For the school district nowadays. It pays benefits."

"Yeah? What do you do?"

"I'm a custodian. Doesn't sound glamorous, but somebody's gotta do it."

"Indeed."

"So," Amber said, getting a little closer and touching Conor's arm with two fingers, "are you still the perpetual bachelor?"

"Actually, no. I'm engaged to be married." Conor looked up from Amber's face and looked around the room. "Morgan's around here somewhere." Making eye contact with her again, he said, "I'd love for you to meet her."

The smile plastered on her face was now saccharine sweet. "Yes, I'd love that."

As if on cue, Morgan showed up at his side and wound an arm around his. "Hey, babe. Sorry I was gone so long." Then, politely and yet with a tinge of possessiveness (she played her part so well), she turned to Amber. "Hi. I'm Morgan Tredway, Conor's fiancée." She even put out her hand for a friendly shake.

Amber seemed reluctant to take her hand but did it anyway—and, after introducing herself, she skedaddled on to greener pastures, saying it was nice to catch up.

Morgan muttered, "Sorry I was slow getting over here."

"Worked out fine."

"But I'm as dry as an ancient whore's panties. Can I get some cash for another drink?"

She'd earned it. Pulling out his wallet, he handed her a credit card. "Go for it."

"You want anything?"

He tilted his glass to draw attention to it. "I'm still working on this one."

"Be right back."

Morgan was doing a great job as his fiancée, so his plan was going off without a hitch. But why was he actually looking at her ass as she made her way to the bar?

It was that damned dress. And she did look sexy as hell in it.

If she wasn't his assistant…

"Conor!" He turned to see another old female classmate. He hadn't remembered her name at the last reunion, but he wouldn't forget it now.

"Hey, Kyra." Although, he realized in retrospect, it would have been off-putting if he'd "forgotten" again. He couldn't help but remember the last reunion, though. She'd twirled a lock of hair in her fingers and said, "Red," because her hair was a deep shade of red only chemicals could properly achieve. "Red equals fire. *Fyra* equals Kyra." And then she'd jutted out her hip and placed her hand on it, making her look like she was posing for a magazine. He hadn't recalled her from high school, and she'd shown him her small class photo in the yearbook—her hair had been a mousy brown and she even looked painfully shy…but she swore the red brought out her true devilish nature.

She'd probably been the most insistent of all the women vying for his attention then, even inviting Conor to her room that night—but he'd made some lame excuse of staying with his parents and not wanting to worry them.

"You remembered this time, you gorgeous hunk of man meat." She sauntered up to him and not only gave him a hug, making sure her breasts pushed into him, but she also kissed him on the cheek. The outfit she wore showed off those ample breasts, and he could tell she was quite proud of them, based on the way she displayed them like prize pumpkins at the county fair. Only instead of Miracle-Gro, she'd likely invested in augmentation surgery. "So I have to assume you're just as successful as you were the last time I saw you—or maybe more?"

Conor wasn't just humble; he also didn't want to encourage this woman when his backup was off filling up her drink. "Doing pretty well. What about you? What have you been up to since the last time we saw each other?"

"After leaving my first husband," she said, leaning in close and lowering her voice, "I started stripping." She began laughing raucously and then added, "Can you believe that?"

Shit. Where the hell was Morgan when he needed her? He didn't want to search her out obviously, thinking that might seem rude, but he was getting desperate. Then he heard another female voice to the side.

"Kyra, you can't go stealing all the available men!"

Conor turned. First, his nose was assaulted by the heavy scent of orchids—too much body spray and too many bodies in a space that became tighter as more drinks were guzzled. Then his eyes took in a woman that filled him with horror deep in his heart. This woman—Patti, he believed he remembered her name was—had black eyebrows obviously filled in with a pencil and lips lined in burgundy but filled in with red.

In short, she looked a hot mess—but it appeared that she *wanted* to look that way.

"Conor!" she screamed. "So damn good to see you. I was afraid you wouldn't be here."

Before he could do a thing, she grabbed him around the waist and hugged him hard, the scent of fake orchids clinging to his shirt. Off in the distance at the bar stood Morgan looking over at him, and he bugged out his eyes at her, hoping she'd get the signal that if he needed her help, now was the time. She shrugged and mouthed something, but then the bartender distracted her and she turned around.

He wanted to dock her pay for that.

But he needed to be polite to his new friends. "Wouldn't want to miss this, would I?"

"Is Kyra boring you with her stripping stories?" As if it were confidential, she said in a low voice, "Mine are better." Then she cackled and Kyra joined in with her.

Conor was praying that someone—anyone—would rescue him, because he was uncomfortable to the core, but he didn't want to hurt any feelings…the whole reason Morgan was supposed to accompany him in the first place.

But he didn't actually need her with him to play that card, did he?

"Well…I'm not sure how my fiancée would feel about you ladies telling me dirty stories."

"*Fiancée?*" Kyra managed to say the word, and Conor struggled to keep a straight face then, because both women's guilty expressions gave away their true intentions. Had they really thought fighting over him would be worth it, that he'd surely choose one of them?

Patti recovered first. "So where is this fiancée of yours? I can't speak for Kyra but I know I'd like to meet her."

"Oh, yes. Me, too."

"Here's your card, honey," Morgan said, her timing almost impeccable. She got on her tiptoes and kissed him on the cheek, and he hoped to God his expression didn't give away that this wasn't normal. She was playing the role beautifully and here he was on the verge of blowing it.

While pulling the wallet out of his pocket, he asked, "What did you get?"

"A pineapple daquiri. Want a taste?"

He held up his Jack and Coke and, on a whim, drained the glass. If the evening was going to continue going this way, he was going to need the drink. "No, thanks. But let me introduce you to some of my old classmates. This is Kyra," he said, nodding at the lady with fiery hair, "and Patti, right?"

"Yes!" Patti beamed—strange that she cared if Conor remembered her, because he was pretty sure their paths hadn't crossed much back in the day. The overly made up woman leaned over and touched Morgan's hand as if they'd been best friends forever and said, "We were over here tryin' to steal your man." She'd said it as a joke, but Conor knew the humor resided in the fact that her statement was completely true.

Conor had no idea how Morgan would react. Would she act like a jealous girlfriend or a cold bitch?

Full of surprises, she wrapped her arm around Conor's waist and grinned. "I can't blame you there. He's the best."

Patti sighed as if she completely agreed, which made Conor almost laugh again, because she really didn't know him. Kyra, though, looked miffed, like she couldn't understand why Conor didn't wait for this reunion to hook up with an available classmate who barely remembered him anyway.

"I'm the lucky one," Conor said. And he meant it.

Liquor made everything better.

Morgan had readjusted her attitude after the first couple of drinks. For some reason, she'd been feeling pissed off at Conor, but she needed to remind herself that she was there *for him*. He was fucking *paying* her to be here—and he was buying the free-flowing drinks on top of it, even though they were outrageously priced. She'd only had three, but her buzz was on hardcore—and if she didn't ease up, she was going to be drunk.

And obnoxious.

He hadn't been kidding, though. The single and newly divorced gals had sniffed him out and were clawing and pawing for a piece of him. And as silly as this whole plan had seemed, she had to admit to herself that it was working. She must have been playing her part well, because the women were rolling away like rain on a freshly waxed car.

But the alcohol was starting to get to her. Maybe that was thanks to the higher altitude.

Conor and five other friends were chatting, talking about their jobs. *Boring.* This was a great excuse to try to sober up a bit. She whispered to Conor that she'd be back—after all, he was with three other guys and two gals, all seemingly taken, so he'd be safe while she asked for a glass of water from the bartender. Maybe even a straight Coke just to try to dilute the liquor she'd consumed.

For supposedly being watered down drinks, the effects were potent, so switching right now was a good idea.

There was a hell of a crowd around the bartender, though. Apparently, everyone here felt like good times were better with a little buzz. Morgan hadn't been much of a drinker since she'd begun working for Conor, but once in a while didn't hurt, right?

A woman with chin-length blonde hair stood next in line (although it was more a fan of people rather than an unorganized queue). She looked familiar to Morgan, but she'd met so many people over the course of the evening that she wouldn't have been able to remember their names, even if she'd written them down—and subtly reading their nametags wasn't working, either.

But, as she stood there, it came to her—this was the first woman who'd hit on Conor this evening.

After the woman got her fresh drink, she turned to scan the room and made eye contact with Morgan. Morgan couldn't tell if her own gaze would look cold or neutral, but even though she was here to keep women from sinking their talons into her boss, she didn't have to be a bitch. "Hi again," she said, trying to keep it friendly.

"You're Conor's fiancée, right?"

"Yes. Morgan. And I'm sorry. What's your name again?"

"Amber."

"Amber. Nice to meet you, Amber. Again." God…she couldn't feel her teeth. That was always the first sign that she'd probably been drinking way too much. And the need to talk a lot was another sign—but that couldn't really be helped. "Are you having fun?"

"Oh, yes. It's always great catching up with people. I see some of these guys on a regular basis, but most of them I haven't seen since our last reunion—unless you count Facebook."

Morgan snort-laughed. "Yeah, but how well do you know what's up with people if you're keeping in touch with them on Facebook really? You'll see pictures of their animals and kids and what they ate for dinner, and you tell them *happy birthday* and *happy anniversary* and celebrate *fake* anniversaries of your online friendship, but how much do you really share with each other there?"

"Lots actually. I message one of my best friends at least once a week—and I don't know what I'd do without her. Plus my mom does a lot of traveling nowadays and it's a good way for me to keep in touch with her. And I keep an eye on my kids, too, and they don't even know it."

"I hadn't thought of that."

An eyebrow arched, Amber replied, "You will when you have kids."

Brr. Morgan forced another smile and looked ahead at the bartender, wondering when the hell he'd take Amber's order. Funny, though, Morgan wasn't feeling as uncomfortable as she might have.

"So how did you and Conor meet anyway?"

Shit. The two of them hadn't discussed any kind of cover story. But maybe the truth was the best way. For all she knew, Conor had already told that to people. "He hired me as his assistant."

"For his accounting business?"

"Yes. I've been there…five years now." A pleasant feeling washed over Morgan, reminding her that the alcohol was still flowing through her veins unimpeded. Anything she drank now wouldn't help that, but at least it would stop her from maybe getting worse.

"What do you do?"

"Keep him organized." No way would she tell this woman her sordid past, that of not actually knowing a thing about being an assistant. "I schedule appointments, gather information and stuff. I meet with clients, too, when it's just a matter of giving them reports and collecting money."

"Will you keep your job after you get married?"

All of a sudden, this gal was her best friend—but Morgan appreciated that, because it passed the time...and it was better than the cattiness that had been going on earlier.

"I don't see why not." Giggling like the drunken crazy woman she was becoming, she added, "You think he could do it without me?"

Amber took a slow sip of her drink. "Well...what did he do *before* he hired you?"

"He survived—but I'm talking the bare minimum, you know? The man was going in twenty different directions and working eighteen-hour days. He needed me to help him get his shit together and take a load off his shoulders."

"Okay, I got that. But I recommend you *stay* there, no matter what. Even if you decide to have kids later...'cause the second you turn your back, he'll be cheating on you, just like all cheating bastard men."

Umm...issues much?

"Yes, lots," Amber said.

"Oh, shit. I said that out loud?"

The other woman started laughing. "That's okay, honey. You're just being honest. I like that. And I bet Conor does, too. But I'm sure you gathered there's a reason why I have those issues. A woman can only take being cheated on for so long before she loses it."

"I got one that'll beat that." Amber raised her eyebrows while taking another sip of her almost-empty drink, giving Morgan the floor. "My boyfriend *just told me* he wanted to break up with me because I wear too much red. And then, the very next day, he was in a—"

"Your *boyfriend?* As in *right now?*" Amber shook her head slowly. "And you're worried about Conor cheating on you?"

Oh, *fuck.* She'd just done that, hadn't she? Spilled the beans?! Fuck, fuck, *fuckity fuck.*

CHAPTER EIGHT

WHAT THE FUCK was Morgan's goddamn damage? Seriously.

She had to think fast—but, fortunately, that was one of her skills, even tipsy.

Would she be able to wriggle out of this one? More importantly, were her lying skills up to par?

"Oh, no. Did I say that happened *now*?" She laughed—a little too hard, but she was inebriated, after all. "No...this happened...*way* in the past. *Before* Conor and I got together. It was the thing that made me look at Conor differently."

God...had she pulled it off? Talk about a remedy for drunkenness. She felt a hell of a lot more sober than the effect two cups of coffee would have had.

"Oh, okay. Yeah, I can see why."

Morgan knew the time for talking was over. There was too much potential for her to say far more incriminating things with her loose lips. Drinking might have made this shindig a little more fun—but now it was dangerous as hell.

"Ma'am? *Ma'am?!*" the bartender asked. When Morgan turned to face him, he asked, "What can I get you?"

She put on as sweet a smile as she could muster before she asked, "Do you have any coffee back there?"

*   *   *

All in all, the evening had gone well. Not only had Conor caught up with a lot of old classmates who reminded him of nothing but good times, all swaddled in nostalgia, but Morgan's presence had managed to (finally) keep the gals at bay. Figuratively, of course. He was still chatting with a good many of them, but he didn't have available females pawing and clawing at him, trying to sink their teeth into his flesh while attempting to assess his net worth based on his suit and business description.

Unfortunately, Patti's horrid perfume had lingered on his jacket all night long. That, and there was no sign of his buddy Steve.

But he had to give Morgan credit. Her presence—and acting abilities—deflected a lot of unwanted attention. He also needed to take a little credit, because the whole thing had been his brilliant idea in the first place. It worked! Now he could enjoy the rest of the time just visiting and having fun.

Morgan excused herself to go to the restroom (making him think she was probably drinking a little too much), and Conor swirled the ice in his drink, downing the last of watered down alcohol. As he set the glass down on a table, the most beautiful girl—now woman—from high school appeared straight ahead.

Raquel Bettis.

She took up his entire frame, looking good enough to eat. Long, flowing blonde hair, just like back then, high cheekbones, exotic eyes—and he bet her legs were still sexy as hell, but she had them hidden underneath a long skirt, and just her hot pink toenails peeked out. She still looked like a million bucks, but, if he wasn't mistaken, her breasts were bigger than before.

Not a bad thing.

Now why didn't a woman like her want him? Why didn't he have a smoking hot Raquel trying to tempt him instead of cringeworthy Kyras and Pattis?

Raquel's smile could just about kill him. White teeth framed by luscious pink lips had his complete attention. "Conor...it's been too long. How have you been?"

Conor took a step toward her, ready to shake her hand. Instead, she wrapped her arms around him, pulling him close. The scent of her musky perfume filled his nostrils, making his blood swirl and replacing the cheap stuff Patti had smothered him with. Raquel's body pressed against his was firm in the right places but soft and feminine in others.

She was the one who got away.

Instead of answering her question, he asked his own. "Raquel, how are you?"

"Better now that I found you."

Most of the women here competing for him now that he had money and no ring on his finger were the ones he wanted to scare off. Raquel, though? He might not mind getting to know the lovely woman she'd become.

"I've had my ups and downs," she said as she let the hug end, leaving her hand on his arm. "You're the one person I'd hoped to see here now."

He questioned it, though, knowing he had to be cautious. After all, his teenage self had been turned down by this woman not once, not twice, but three times. And Raquel had been "happily married" at their ten-year reunion. So she was thrilled to see him now. Really? "Why is that?"

She squeezed his arm, licking her lips as if ready to devour him. "Because I think you're the yummiest man here."

Morgan arrived on his other side, wrapping her arm through his before getting on her tiptoes and kissing his cheek. "Hi!" she chirped, sounding more cheerful than was her norm. "My name's Morgan. I'm Conor's fiancée. And you are?"

Suddenly, the temperature of Raquel's hand through Conor's jacket felt as if it were covered in ice—but she kept it in place. After introducing herself, she said, "Conor and I had a few classes together back in the day."

"That's nice." The way Morgan gripped his arm possessively almost made him believe they were truly engaged. "Conor and I have a honeymoon planned for Hawaii."

"Oh…which island?"

This was the point where he expected Morgan to falter, but she didn't miss a beat. "We talked about the main island, but I'd love to spend time on Maui."

"You really need to check out Lanai. It's my favorite."

Morgan arched a dark eyebrow. "We might…but I suspect we're going to be spending a lot of time in the hotel room. We won't have time to see everything."

What the hell was that vicious purr coming out of Morgan's mouth? It was kind of a turn on…almost made him *want* to be her fiancé. Crazy.

Raquel cleared her throat—her neck was still lovely after all these years. "Well, it was nice to meet you, Maureen."

"Morgan."

"Oh, yes, Morgan. Sorry. Conor, really good to see you again." The corners of her lips twitched up. "Maybe I'll see you around over the weekend."

"I'll be here."

As Raquel walked away, he recognized the way she sashayed her hips like she used to, emphasizing her gorgeous ass, and Conor couldn't help himself—but why should he? It wasn't like he was *really* engaged. "You still look amazing, Raquel."

She turned around, a devious grin eating up her entire face. "Thank you, Conor. I think you look even better."

No ego boost was needed, but Conor would be lying to himself if he said he hadn't enjoyed it. As Raquel touched another man's arm nearby, Conor felt Morgan's fingers gripping his like a vice. "You seriously like that dumb bimbo?"

He could feel a scowl wrinkling his brow. "Careful, Morgan. There are plenty of people around here with great hearing."

"And I don't care who hears. She was trying to steal *my man*. That makes her a stupid fucking bimbo."

Conor could have felt embarrassed about her language, the volume of her voice, the cattiness of her tone—but, instead, it somehow made him feel masculine and proud. Two beautiful women were almost fighting over him.

He could get used to this shit.

Morgan had just about had all the fun she could stand. These folks weren't *that* much older than she, but they had nothing in common. Most of them were nice enough, introducing themselves, asking about how she and Conor had met, regaling her with the occasional story from their high school days, but she was starting to feel out of her element—and *bored.*

Fortunately, the alcohol helped, even if too much.

After a cup of coffee, she'd discovered that her buzz was short-lasting and the ennui set in again. She chatted with the bartender and asked him for something with less alcohol. He suggested one of his specialties, a drink he called *Hawaiian Sunset*. Immediately, she was drawn to the name, imagining sitting on the beach somewhere on one of the islands, relaxing with a refreshing beverage while the sun slowly dropped below the horizon to the west.

On *Maui*, Raquel. Fuck Lanai.

The bartender had told her the beverage had pineapple rum and a bunch of other stuff, and she was sold. Conor was paying for the drinks—and, as the night had worn down and the crowd had thinned out, a couple of staff made rounds a few times—and they had no issues with fetching her glass to bring back a full one.

Once she got back to buzzed—without feeling full-on drunk—she again found the situation easy to justify…because she wouldn't have been here to begin with if not for Conor. Once in a while, new folks would breeze by and he'd introduce them, but she knew she'd never remember their names. After two hours of standing with him while plastering on a rubbery smile, she was done playing…especially because she was sick and fucking tired of hearing from his comedic classmates how he'd "robbed the cradle."

Like she was a little kid or something.

Fuck those old farts.

That thought made her giggle so hard, she couldn't stop.

Hmm. Maybe the alcohol *was* having an effect again.

And Conor was closer than she'd thought. "You okay, honey?"

They were standing next to two men but Morgan had wandered away a few feet, apparently still within hearing distance. "Never better, stud muffin." Calling her boss something bordering on inappropriate sent her into another gale of laughter.

"Maybe I need to get you back to our room."

"I'm *fine*," she said, realizing she probably needed to cut herself off once more. One more drink could cause her to lose control of her tongue and brain muscles—and that could ruin this whole plan. She didn't need another spilling-the-beans Amber-type moment. "I just need to go to the ladies' room."

Her feet weren't as steady as they should have been on those heels, but she sucked down a deep breath and smoothed out her skirt before smiling at her fake fiancé and his friends. Conor asked, "You sure you don't need any help, honey?"

Honey? That was almost funny. "Yeah, I got it, babe." He had a concerned expression, which almost made her start cackling again—but she managed to make it to the hallway without wobbling or giggling maniacally. She wandered down the hall, ready to begin cursing because she just wanted to fucking pee, for Christ's sake, and then she found the door. She wandered in and took the free stall down the way next to the one that accommodated wheelchairs. After locking the door, she took a deep breath and then sat down on the toilet.

There was a flush, followed by another, and, as Morgan heard water begin running into the sink, she relaxed enough to do her business.

"So, Brenda, how many guys here are still hot enough to bang, you think?"

"Oh, God. Not enough."

"I know, right?" Morgan could hear the rhythmic chug of someone cranking on the paper towel dispenser, working out a length long enough to dry the woman's hands.

"How many of these guys have gone bald, for God's sake?"

The other woman—not Brenda—let out a cackle worthy of the Wicked Witch of the West. "And don't get me started on their beer bellies and pasty skin." Both women let out a peal of laughter. "They probably have corns on their feet."

Holy shit. Morgan recognized that catty fucking voice.

"And limp dicks. They probably have prescriptions for Viagra."

"I know, right?"

Yeah, that had to be Raquel.

"Did you see Randy? I promise you, girlfriend, all the Viagra in the world couldn't help that man out."

Another howl of laughter.

God, they were bitches. Morgan had long since finished peeing, but no way was she coming out of there. She wouldn't be able to contain the look of disgust on her face. Maybe she had a potty mouth—and maybe she'd been thinking similar thoughts—but she hoped she wasn't as catty as these two.

"I hate this lipstick."

"It looks good on you."

"The color's great, but it won't stay on."

"Here, use this." Morgan heard the clink of plastic rolling

around the ceramic bowl of the sink, followed by giggles. Maybe those two had had too much to drink as well. "This is a twenty-four hour stain. Lasts through multiple blow jobs."

More cackles.

Oh, Jesus. Now she wouldn't be able to even look at Raquel without picturing a limp dick in her mouth. At the thought, Morgan felt her mouth start to widen, ready to burst into giggles herself, and she clapped her hands over her lips.

Cum-guzzling cow.

Fuck. She pressed her hands even harder against her mouth.

"What do you think?"

"Looks good, especially against the ocean blue of your dress."

After a few moments of silence, Morgan began to wonder if they'd snuck out and she simply hadn't heard them leave. Just as she got ready to pull some tissue off the toilet paper roll, she heard Raquel's voice pitched lower than it had been. "So have you run into Conor Hammond yet?"

"No. He's here?"

"God, girl. You have *got* to find him. Hot…not like high school or even last reunion. Swear to God I'd do him in a minute."

"Seriously?"

"Oh, yeah." Their voices began to fade as their heels clicked on the tile. "Except for he's engaged now and the fiancée's with him."

"Like that's ever stopped you before."

More squawking as the door settled back into its closed position.

Why the fuck was Morgan starting to feel jealous for real? Was she such a great actress that she was starting to think like a real fiancée?

Flush.

By the time they walked in the door to their hotel room, Morgan was feeling sober. Through the entire last half hour of the evening, she'd sat at a table, struggling to keep her head up and eyes open, but now she leaned her head on the wall of the elevator, ready to sleep. After getting to their floor, though, she found her second wind.

She wasn't going to tell Conor about the conversation between faceless Brenda and phony Raquel, but she had plenty of questions. "So tell me about Rachel." The bitch would never know she'd decimated her name like she'd done to Morgan's face about her own, but it made her feel better anyway.

"I see what you did there." Conor slid the card in the lock. "Long story, Morgan."

As the door clicked closed and Conor flipped the metal lock at the top, she pulled off her heels. "Well, I'm glad you cleared that up. After all, we're so busy, I don't know how the fuck we could ever find time to chat."

Conor chuckled but Morgan couldn't tell if he was actually amused or just putting up with her as he often did. All these years of working for him, and while she didn't give a flying fuck, it would be nice at this moment to know he really liked her.

But that wasn't Morgan's schtick. She didn't give a shit.

So why did she now?

"You really want to hear this?"

"I asked, didn't I?"

She flopped down in the overstuffed beige chair and rubbed her feet. When was the last time she'd worn heels like these? Sure, her legs looked awesome in them, but she hadn't realized till she'd removed them that they'd been pure torture on her toes.

Conor took off his jacket and unbuttoned his cuffs. Damn…those stupid fucking women had helped her remember the truth. Morgan's boss really *was* hot, even if he was quite a bit older than she. And holding onto him, she realized he had a rock-hard body and smelled delicious.

Not like her stupid dipshit ex who smelled like patchouli and pot…Conor smelled like sandalwood and money.

For fuck's sake—she had to stop this.

Right. Now.

"Raquel Bettis…she was in every single English class I had. She wasn't the smartest cookie, but she was sassy, and I liked that about her. Like when we were having a class discussion about the Sherlock Holmes story, 'The Red-Headed League.' You ever read that one?"

"Maybe? I don't remember."

"So these criminals are digging through one shop into a bank vault next door to steal some coins, if I recall correctly, but the teacher was pissed because none of us had much to say about it in class the next day. She asked if any of us wondered where they took all the dirt they'd dug from the tunnel. I hadn't thought much about it, even though it was a logical question. Raquel, though." Conor's lopsided smile made Morgan think he'd probably been a good-looking boy back in the day. "'Who cares?' she said. 'It was just dirt. If it was important to the story, wouldn't this *esteemed author* have included it?' Mrs. Kramer was so frustrated with her—but Raquel was well-loved by everyone, the principal included, so the teacher dropped the textbook on the desk and gave us more reading homework that night and threatened us, saying if we weren't ready for a real discussion the next day, she was going to fail us all."

Morgan was not impressed. Granted, she might have said something similar in class, but she was no Raquel fan.

"Then, when Mrs. Kramer turned to the board, Raquel rolled her eyes and flipped her off half-heartedly—and that made everyone laugh. When Mrs. K. turned around and assigned more homework without raising her voice, Raquel rolled her eyes again and didn't say anything else—but she winked at me, and I fell in love."

"You fell in love with *her*? She's a bitch."

"Maybe, but I hadn't had a girl give me the time of day. That was the first time a female had even flirted with me."

"I doubt that, Conor."

"You didn't know me back then. I was the epitome of a nerd. Girls didn't just ignore me—they avoided me like the plague. Probably afraid I'd get science fiction cooties on them."

"Maybe they didn't know that accounting pays."

"Seriously, Morgan…even the geeky girls didn't pay any attention to me." She couldn't help but cock her eyebrow. Were they completely blind? "Have you not seen any pictures of me in high school? Guess I'm gonna have to take you back to my parents' house." Conor hung his jacket in the closet by the door before sitting in a chair. "I was the stereotype—glasses, zits, wimpy arms."

"You're full of shit."

"I'm dead serious. And Raquel winking at me gave me the confidence to talk to her at the beginning of class each day after that. Then she started asking me every morning about the reading assignments."

"So you helped that twit pass English class?"

Nodding, he said, "Yeah, but she was capable."

Remembering her comment in the bathroom about blow jobs, Morgan said, "I highly doubt that."

As if he hadn't heard a word, he added, "I was smitten after that. I helped one of the fab four in the pom-pom squad graduate high school."

"And she didn't give you the time of day."

Conor nodded. "Yeah, not back then. None of the girls did. It was almost like I didn't exist—unless someone needed homework help. And I didn't complain. Any attention is better than nothing, right?"

Morgan shrugged. "I think I'd rather be a wallflower than be anywhere near those cum-guzzling bitches."

"Bitch*es*?" Conor asked, emphasizing the plural while completely ignoring the nasty description.

"Gal named Brenda?"

"Oh, Brenda. Yeah, she was part of Raquel's four-pack."

"You only had four cheerleaders for your whole school?"

"No…there were probably twenty or thirty divided among all the squads. But there were three girls who were Raquel wannabes and followed her around like lapdogs. They even talked to me, thanks to her."

"Because you were giving her what she *wanted*, Conor. I'm no rocket scientist and even I know that shit."

Conor shook his head and sat on the couch. "You're pretty and snappy, Morgan. You'd never understand what a nerd like me had to go through back in the day."

The laughter roared out of her mouth. "*Back in the day?* Like you're an old grandpa now."

"You know what I mean."

And then it dawned on her—he'd called her *pretty*.

Did he really mean that?

Her brain couldn't even ponder the concept when he'd begun talking again. "When I went off to college, I found myself. I found my confidence, because for the first time I was judged for my brains and not my looks or who I hung out with. After being ignored all through high school, I became comfortable in my own skin and never looked back."

Still shell-shocked, Morgan tried to keep her words neutral. "The way it should be."

"But my ten-year reunion reminded me of all those old emotions. You'd understand if you'd gone to your reunion."

"Yeah, we already went through all that. It's bullshit, Conor."

"I'm paying you to say otherwise." Morgan rolled her eyes but said nothing, because he was technically right. As he unbuttoned the top of his shirt, he continued. "Raquel was married at that reunion, to a guy in oil who made millions of dollars and she was his trophy wife. I think they had one kid maybe. Doesn't matter, though. She hung on his arm like the diamonds hung on her neck, and I figured she was set for life. Just like high school, she barely talked to me—but she gave me a quick wink across the room."

"Just like the bitch she is." Why the hell was there some green-eyed monster stirring in her belly?

"Doesn't matter, Mo. The teenage boy in me is feeling like David against Goliath. All the star football players look like old men and it's not like our ten-year, where I felt like the women were just attracted to my money. Now I feel like they like me for *me*."

Bitches. Fucking cunty bitches. *I have always liked Conor for his insides.* She was loyal and starting to look at him through a new lens, but she realized she had no claim to him in that regard. Instead, she had a duty to him. She was there to help him, to be his right-hand woman, just like she always was at the office. "So do you want me to make Raquel and all the other women jealous as hell?"

Just like I'm starting to feel?

"Yeah. I think I'd like that."

Only tomorrow would tell if Morgan felt the same way...or if she was getting ready to put up a fight.

CHAPTER NINE

THE NEXT MORNING, Morgan had a slight headache—but nothing a couple of ibuprofen tablets wouldn't take care of. Except she remembered something...something she needed to let Conor know about.

He was working out, so she just had to wait for him to get back. She should be exercising, too, but that wasn't happening. This damned reunion had completely messed up her entire routine. She hadn't made a to-do list this morning, nor had she been working out like she would have been back at home. Reminding herself that she'd get back on track once she returned, she decided to jump in the shower to get a start on the day.

Her makeup was on and she was dressed and blow drying her hair in the main area when Conor got back. And she felt even more like a heel, because he had two cups of Starbucks in hand.

"Mocha latte," he said, setting it on the table after she'd shut off the dryer.

"Thanks so much, Conor." She lifted the cup to her lips. "How's your morning?"

"Great. But I think I should ask you how *you're* feeling. You had quite a bit to drink last night."

"I'm okay." It was true since the pain reliever had kicked in.

"Brunch starts in half an hour, so I'm going to shower and then we can head down." Conor started walking toward the bathroom.

"Uh...just a second, Conor."

"Yeah?"

"Do you mind sitting down for a minute?"

He had a slight frown on his lips but he nodded his head before joining her at the table. "What's up?"

"Um…you know that Amber woman?"

"Yeah—probably better than you do."

"Very funny. Well…last night, when I was talking to her, I might have accidentally blown your cover."

He drew in a slow breath through his nostrils before saying, "What happened?"

"I can't remember exactly—and I think I recovered okay—but I mentioned something about breaking up with my boyfriend."

The frown made its way to Conor's brow. "How did you recover?"

"I just told her that happened a long time ago before you and I got together…and I think she bought it."

Shaking his head, he asked, "What am I gonna do with you?"

"Marry me for real. That'll throw them off the scent."

"A little extreme, don't you think?" Conor stood and headed back toward the bathroom. "I'll be ready in a bit."

Whew.

As if on death row, Conor and Morgan walked down the hall toward the elevator. He'd been a little pissed at first when Morgan had told him she'd already blabbed to Amber about their little charade, but he blamed himself for not cutting Morgan off the alcohol.

But he'd sensed her boredom and she was being a hell of a good sport, all things considered.

Something else niggled at his brain, though. Morgan, in her usual flippant style of retorting, told him to marry her "for real." Why the hell had he been dwelling on that notion ever since she'd said that?

First of all, Conor didn't plan to marry till he was in his forties—if ever. Second of all, Morgan was his friend—and his assistant, which would make even thinking about crossing that line highly appropriate.

But his brain was mulling the thought anyway.

Stupid.

By the time they got to the first floor, Conor had pressed those ideas to the back of his brain and held the elevator door for Morgan once it slid open. Now he was once again consumed with the reunion and looked down at his shirt, second guessing himself. He had no issues with navy blue, but...

"Conor, would you quit worrying?" Morgan asked, running her hand over his chest and stomach, smoothing the shirt—not that it needed it. He was wearing the damn thing like a woman would pour herself into skin-tight jeans. "You look fucking hot— like let's-serve-you-up-on-a-platter-with-nothing-but-a-fig-leaf-over-your-manhood hot." Conor raised his eyebrows as she squinted her eyes. "This will get their attention."

But he was wearing a workout shirt. How unprofessional would that look?

As if she could hear his thoughts, Morgan said, "It's *brunch*, Conor. And half of these motherfuckers are going to have hangovers the size of Texas, okay?"

Glancing at his pretend betrothed, he noted that she looked gorgeous, and the sunglasses made her look almost like a celebrity as they made their way out of the elevator. She had the air of someone entitled, at any rate—not that Morgan had ever acted that way. Right now, though, she was playing the part of a girlfriend claiming stakes to her man.

He had to admit, even if only to himself, that he totally loved it. As much as he'd loved Raquel's attention in high school English class, he even more loved how Morgan acted possessive now.

He could get used to this.

And why the hell was he starting to think of her as a *real* girlfriend and not just his faithful employee doing his bidding?

"If you say so."

"This is more real," Morgan said, grabbing his hand in hers. "Engaged couples touch each other."

He couldn't argue with her.

"And if you want those bitches eating out of the palm of your hand, you need them to see you're desirable and unavailable."

Without another word, they walked down the cool interior of the looming hotel and followed the signs—back to the ballroom where they'd been the evening before, but this time there was a steamtable full of hot breakfast food and the smell of bacon was heavy.

It looked like the trays of eggs had been untouched. Not shocking, considering all the alcohol that had been guzzled last night. What *was* a bit of a surprise, though, was how many of his former classmates were sipping on mimosas.

Maybe it made them feel better about who they were now.

"Where do you want to sit, Morgan?"

Her voice was low, so he leaned over to hear her better—and he realized it instantly made them appear to be more intimate. "Not like there's a lot of choice, but if you want bitches to be jealous, we need to be near the center. And I can put on a great show. I say we sit right there." His eyes followed her finger to a large round table in the middle of the room, not too far from the large buffet.

There were already two couples there and two men alone, but Conor wasn't about to argue with his right-hand woman. "Lead the way, my dear."

Where the hell had *that* come from?

The grimace on her face told him she was wondering the same damn thing.

Once they got to the table, Morgan grabbed the pitcher of water and poured some into the glasses in front of their seats. The condensation told him the pitchers had been there a while—but the plates in front of their table mates made it look like they'd just barely sat down. "Are these seats taken?"

Morgan had already staked their claim, so heaven help them if one of these folks said they had to go elsewhere.

"No, go for it," said one of the single men.

The other guy without a date said, "You look familiar."

"Crap. I forgot my nametag. Sorry."

"Guess no breakfast for you!" The large woman to the right started snorting and laughing raucously, making Conor fear she would explode with a heart attack if she didn't chill.

"I'm Conor Hammond. This is my fiancée, Morgan Tredway."

Unusually subdued, Morgan nodded and smiled. How odd.

After the whole table went through polite introductions, he said, "What can I get you to drink, darling?"

Where the hell were these crazy terms of endearment coming from? It was so not like him, and he expected Morgan to give him hell later. "These mimosas look amazing—but I'm craving coffee. Could you bring me a cup, please?"

"How about both?"

This was the woman who made and fetched him coffee every morning, even though it was completely out of character for her—and now he was waiting on her hand and foot…as if he were truly a doting fiancé.

He scoped out the room and decided to focus on coffee first. There were two huge urns on a table against the wall behind the steamy buffet, along with pitchers of juice and water. After he'd grabbed two coffee cups and cozied up to the caffeinated urn, he sensed a warm body to his right.

Lovely Raquel with her long blonde hair and a short pink dress put him in the mind of a mermaid. There was no particular reason why he thought that, except that maybe her flowing hair looked somewhat like the lady on the Starbucks cups Morgan fetched every so often, like the one he'd brought to her earlier that morning. "Fancy meeting you here," Raquel all but whispered, cocking her head in a way that seemed to make her eyes sparkle.

Conor was certain Morgan's plan was already working. Raquel had never seemed so interested in him. "How did you sleep last night?"

"Not too bad. But I had the naughtiest dreams."

"Oh, really?" Did Conor hear her right?

Raquel giggled and touched his arm, reminding him of the way she'd flirted with her football player boyfriends back in high school. "I'll have to tell you about them later." Winking, she breezed off, leaving behind the scent of feminine musk.

Conor felt his brow furrow as he pulled on the tab of the coffee urn, filling the white ceramic mug with the steamy, earthy liquid. Over the past ten-plus years, he'd slowly built up his company and the past five had shown amazing growth. That hadn't happened because he'd been a boy on the verge of popping a hard-on just because a sexy woman had smirked and batted her eyelashes his way. It had been because he'd become a take-control man. He'd had a vision and been able to see his way clearly through the forest to the finish line. He hadn't had women distracting the shit out of him—and it was that take-charge attitude that would carry him through. If he allowed himself to once more be the nerdy high school version of himself, not only would he have no chance to win the woman, but he'd have to struggle to get back on top.

He'd become that confident, in-control man before Morgan had come along. He could do it again and conquer she who'd previously been unobtainable. He had to admit that Morgan's help was nice, though. Playing the jealous girlfriend could only help things along, but he had to don an asshole persona, much like the alpha male football players had done back in the day.

Why did women like assholes?

It didn't matter, but he could enjoy the benefits of playing one. He vowed at that moment that he would have Raquel Bettis before the weekend was over. The former cheerleader sat at a table with the woman he remembered as Brenda Sterling before she looked his way again and smiled before blowing him a kiss.

Yeah...this might actually be easy.

The reunion committee, partly led by overly perky Kendra King, had a *Memories* segment slide show that morning. Perhaps they'd sensed the hangovers that would ensue after the cocktail event from the previous evening, or maybe they'd expected there would be low attendance that morning, so why not do something low key? Whatever the case, the diners got to enjoy a PowerPoint version of their freshman yearbook, along with Kendra's nonstop commentary. It had been amusing at first but Morgan was just about ready to go back to bed. There was no way in hell she'd be able to keep her eyes open during the golfing event of the afternoon.

What made it all the more unbearable was that Conor was acting strangely. It was as if a pod person had stolen his body the night before, but she suspected Conor had donned a persona that would make him feel more comfortable around his old classmates. As she observed him that morning, though, she began to think it was a move to impress the ladies...and that was fine. That was the whole point, right? Keep away the ones he didn't want so the more desirable ones could approach. But that didn't change the fact that her old boss and friend was nowhere to be found. She didn't care much for this shallow version of Conor, so more than once, she asked if he was okay. He tried to assure her by saying,

"Of course, I am. Why wouldn't I be?"

But his words didn't assure her at all.

Near the end of the dreadful slideshow, Morgan noticed that Conor was watching another table across the way—and wouldn't you know? The table held the equally dreadful bleach blonde bimbo Raquel, a mean girl if Morgan had ever known one. Somehow, Conor couldn't see it at all, instead enamored with the woman's enormous flirting powers that were proving to be his Kryptonite. He had no defense against her.

It was so strange. Her Conor—suave, smooth, confident Conor—would have been impervious to her charms. But, of course, they'd gone back in time.

Maybe Morgan would have to say something about it later— but she'd have to tread lightly. She didn't want to bruise his ego, especially right now when it might be particularly fragile.

At least the banal slideshow meant she hadn't had to engage in painfully dull conversation with the folks around her table. Some of these guys *felt* old—not like they were approaching middle age but instead like they were feebly racing toward the nursing home. It made her grateful that her boss seemed so much younger than a lot of them. And how had he escaped that mentality?

Grinning, she gave herself a little credit for that…for keeping him on his toes.

But his preoccupation with that old hag Raquel was becoming disconcerting.

Suddenly, Conor turned toward her. Yeah, he could've blamed it on the end of the presentation, but she'd seen where his eyes had truly been. She doubted he'd absorbed anything on the screen. Rather than say a word, Morgan raised her eyebrows in anticipation of what he planned to say.

Conor leaned over the table and Morgan responded. Why had she never noticed the spicy, delicious cologne he wore before this weekend? She caught notes of sandalwood and citrus, making her mouth water more than the strawberries she'd consumed minutes earlier.

What the fuck was wrong with her?

"Have you been paying attention?"

"To what?" she asked, wondering what the hell was irritating him now.

Leaning farther forward, Conor pressed his lips into her hair.

She could feel his warm breath on her ear, causing a shiver to dart down her spine, reminding her that she was, in fact, susceptible to masculine charms, even if they were from her boss and not her usual flavor of man. His voice reverberated against her eardrum, its low tone touching multiple nerves throughout her body. "That guy sitting with Raquel? That's Jacob Martin, our star quarterback two years in a row. Helped us win state our senior year. He dated a string of cheerleaders but never her—and now he's apparently going to win in that department, too."

Morgan pulled back enough to look in his face and, oh, his brown eyes. So beautiful. Why had she never noticed how gorgeous his eyes were before? But they were less attractive with him seeing green. "Why are you letting it bother you, Conor?"

Several beats passed before he blinked and swallowed. "Because this was supposed to be *my* time. Jacob's washed up. I'm only just now coming in to my stride."

"That's true," she agreed. But why the fuck would he want to take a woman like Raquel, likely infected with chlamydia and syphilis, along for the ride? "So what the fuck are you gonna do, boss?"

The way he masked his sigh like he often did back at the office reminded Morgan how much he hated her casual way of dropping the F-bomb whenever it suited her. But she didn't intend to apologize at this moment, because there were far more pressing matters at hand. Conor evidently wasn't going to answer, because he raised his eyebrows before picking up his glass and downing half the mimosa in one straight shot.

"I'm going to go over there and talk to them both."

Suddenly, the thought of Conor with Raquel raced through her mind. *No.* It wasn't because she'd discovered a newfound (and unusual) appreciation of her boss of late—it was because Raquel was a man-eater, and the woman was on the prowl for a new guy. Morgan didn't want her friend to be the victim of Raquel's self-absorbed obsession. She'd known far too many women just like her—the love 'em and leave 'em type. Sure, they might play around with a guy like Conor, making him feel great while she used him for his money or his power, but she wouldn't stick around long if he hid the wallet.

But there was also another problem. A mean Raquel type, if she had no interest in a guy like Conor, would have no issues shaming him, either—so, for example, if he did try to insert himself between the flirting conversation of Raquel and Jacob, Conor might get told off and be left humiliated, even if he had no emotional stake in it.

Morgan would have none of that. She'd been protecting her boss's reputation since she'd begun working for him, and he was paying her overtime right now.

"Wait, Conor," she said, her eyes laser-focused on his. "That won't work with a woman like Raquel."

"*What* won't work?"

Morgan drew in a slow breath, wondering how the hell Conor had ever made it this far in life with such sucky social skills. Of course, he hadn't. This wasn't the real Conor here—this was his kid self, and he was in a weird position at the moment, having forgotten how to use the adaptive abilities he'd learned as an adult. It was like he was a dumb geeky teenager again, drooling after the girl he could never have.

But Conor *could* have her—he was good enough.

"The direct approach." Lowering her voice again, she got close to his ear. "That won't work with a woman like Raquel. She expects all men to worship her and do whatever she bids."

"Come on, Morgan. We're adults now."

"Yeah, but look at her, Conor. Do you think she's ever been told *no* a day in her life?" Morgan would bet her bottom fucking dollar that the woman didn't even know the meaning of that word—it would be like a foreign language. She was used to receiving what she wanted—on a silver platter and ASAP. Conor got ready to answer Morgan and she said, "Trust me. She hasn't. And if you go over there and tell her you're a better choice than that washed up football player, she'll grind you like a bug under that ridiculous silver stiletto she's wearing."

Fortunately, her boss was a man of reason. "So what do you propose I do?"

There was no stopping the smirk spreading across her face. "You do what we planned to do when we got here. Only instead of deflecting her, you make her jealous. Make her want you. *Then* she'll be eating out of the palm of your hand."

"Well, playing my fiancée hasn't helped so far, so what now?"

Morgan arched an eyebrow. "You do what any fiancée would do: you *kiss* me…and then wait."

CHAPTER TEN

CONOR SEARCHED MORGAN'S jade green eyes, assessing her intent. This was the kind of silly thing she'd say just to get him to fall for a joke and, when he agreed, she'd pull the rug out from under him—but he was seeing no sign that she was being a smart ass.

"You're serious."

"Yes, dammit. I'm dead serious."

Before he could even decide how to make his move, Morgan wrapped her hand around his neck and pulled his face closer to hers. Why the hell had he never noticed how good she smelled up close before? Her perfume was reminiscent of cloves and cinnamon and other spices, almost making him want to take a bite out of her neck.

But she wasn't giving him a chance.

Instead, she brought her lips close to his, near enough that he could feel little charges of electricity jumping from her mouth to his, pulling him in as if by some mysterious gravitational force.

It made his mouth water.

Made him forget everything else.

When she pressed her lips into his, he kept reminding himself that he was supposed to act like they did this all the time, like it was no big deal—and that should have been easy, considering Morgan was simply working for him.

Except this was so different.

Suddenly, as he inched his tongue inside her mouth, finding

himself desiring her down deep in his loins, he had no thought of ex-cheerleader-what's-her-face. Instead, it was all about the woman who was suddenly in his arms, pressed up against his body.

For the first time in his life, he felt like he had another purpose. Morgan was most certainly not the kind of woman who needed protecting, but he wanted to shelter her anyway. And she definitely wasn't the kind of girl who would need to be told how beautiful and special she was—and yet he now had a deep burning desire to do just that.

In Morgan's words, what the fuck was going on with him?

She tasted sweet and feminine, igniting a yearning deep inside Conor, one that made him want to taste every inch of her, explore her every soft curve.

Kisses were supposed to make *women* breathless, leave the man looking something like James Dean or Marlon Brando back in the fifties—and yet he felt as though she'd knocked *him* down with a bowling ball.

He opened his eyes, praying he looked like the man he'd become and not like nerdy fourteen-year-old Conor, the kid with the big glasses, shiny braces, and egg head. He hoped he now appeared like the confident businessman who knew his shit when it came to money and his ability to make small businesses stronger so they could focus on what they did best.

Morgan's tiny smile injected him with a shot of confidence. But then she ran her hand down to his chest and patted it. "The one thing I hadn't thought of was how to find out if that worked."

Proud of how masculine his voice said, he kept his smile to a minimum. "Isn't that what I pay you for?"

"Let's just assume it did. And I'll start being more handsy with you. If she's hanging around you more tonight, we'll know it worked." Morgan dropped her hands from his chest, and he tried not to feel disappointed about that—after all, it was just a ruse, right? "And if she still seems like she's plugged in somewhere else, I'll start filling her head with all kinds of shit."

"Like what?"

"Like telling her how good you are in bed and stuff like that."

"*What?*"

"Just trust me." Before he could say another word, Morgan started walking off, and Conor felt his kidneys and liver fall through his legs and into his feet, a feeling of nausea replacing the sickening sense of weightlessness—because he was certain she was going to start that crap right now. Instead, she walked over to the coffee urn and began pouring herself another cup.

But he was the one swallowing a large gulp.

Holy fuck. Was that chemistry or just something fucking strange going on? What in holy hell was wrong with her?

Morgan had kissed plenty of men in her day, but she could say none of them had felt or tasted quite like that. Was it because she'd taken control of that moment? Usually in the past, she'd acquiesced and waited for the man to make the initial move but, in this case, time had been of the essence and she'd been inspired.

And it had worked!

As she'd walked back from the coffee urn to their table, she'd caught Raquel's eyes looking first at Conor and then at her—so, in typical Morgan fashion, she waved at the snatch. *Ha.*

But that kiss had been way better than it had had a right to be…and it was going to be hard to think of Conor in any other fashion now.

An hour later and the reunion folks were giving everyone a tour of the high school, showing them all the changes that had been made to the building in the past two decades. According to Conor, they now had a new auditorium and gymnasium, making him wonder why they hadn't just built a new school altogether.

They hadn't even moved into the new wing when Raquel and the quarterback joined them. Raquel started talking to Conor, wriggling her arm in his and just being all-around obnoxious. If Morgan had been a fighter, she would have pulled Raquel outside by her hair.

Instead, she decided that two could play that game.

"Jacob, right?"

Nodding, the older man gave her a slight smile. "Yep, that's it. And you're Conor's fiancée?"

"I am," she said, trying not to look at the Conor-Raquel pairing—and failing miserably.

"Not much longer, am I right?" Jacob's stupid comment wouldn't have been so bad had he not punctuated it with a jab in Morgan's ribs with his elbow. Morgan glanced at him and gave him the best smile she could, but even without seeing herself, she knew it was pinched. The man she was stuck with wasn't too terribly bad. He'd maintained an athletic body, even if his mullet-like haircut seemed a little dated. "I can show you a good time if you get tired of playing third wheel."

She didn't want this guy continuing to entertain the thought that she'd even consider him. "Look, dude, even if I'm pissed at Conor for the moment, he's also my boss—so I can't just dump him. Besides, they're only catching up. It's been ten years, right?"

As the crowd slowed so they could be updated on the financing of the newest wing of the school, Raquel moved her arm so she could rub Conor's lower back. By now, Morgan was seething, but she couldn't say shit about it. Out of the corner of his mouth, Jacob said, "Catching up on *what*?"

Morgan tried to keep her sigh as muffled as possible and pretended to be listening to the babbling up front. That was great that they got a grant so they saved a couple of mil on the addition. Now can we please move on?

As they started moving again—*finally*—Jacob asked, "So how long have you and Conor been together?"

Time for another lie that she hoped they wouldn't get caught in. So long as nobody asked her and Conor the same questions—and, chances were, the curiosity would fizzle out once the reunion was over—she'd be fine. So she was going to make up a story that would be easy to repeat and hard to verify. "I'm not sure. I've been working for him for around five years now...and somewhere in the middle, we became interested in each other. I'm not sure when we actually started dating."

"So you're not one of these women who has a first-date anniversary?"

Morgan peered at a glass display they were walking past but knew she'd have to answer his question. Fortunately, she could utilize honesty here. "No, that's asinine."

"I happen to agree. I can't remember days like that—and I don't need two anniversaries to forget instead of one."

They continued walking down the hall, listening to Kendra and cohorts babble on about all the changes in the building, plus a long-winded discussion about how credit hours had changed over the years, and Morgan thought Jacob finally got the hint to leave her alone.

At least he'd distracted her from the mind-numbing school talk.

Out of the blue, though, Jacob got close to her again. "So where did *you* go to school?"

She could no longer hold her tongue. "You really wanna fuckin' know?"

"Ah…I love a feisty woman."

Morgan stopped walking and didn't care that people were pissed that they had to walk around them. "Dude, you're way too old for me, okay? So just stop hitting on me."

The guy let out an embarrassed laugh and lowered his voice. "I'm not hitting on you. I'm just trying to be friendly. It's not my fault that the person I *wanted* to catch up with has stolen your fiancé and isn't giving me the time of day anymore."

Jacob started to move away and then Morgan felt like a real asshole. He was right, after all. "Jacob…I'm sorry. I guess I *am* a little upset and was taking it out on you." He didn't look convinced and seemed like he was ready to give her a throwaway answer, just as she'd been doing to him moments before. "Friends?" Morgan thrust her hand out, waiting for him to shake it. God, why did some men seem to openly pout when spurned? But he finally took her hand. "You're right. We have something in common—so maybe we *can* enjoy each other's company." Or flirt and try to get her pretend fiancée to give her the time of day…but she wasn't going to hold her breath. Conor finally had Raquel's attention and he didn't seem ready to give it up anytime soon.

Conor had never liked golf, so why the hell was he here? He could play the game okay, but he hated the long boring periods of waiting, even though the walking wasn't so bad. Some of the guys rode in the golf carts, but when moving your feet was the only exercise you got with the game, Conor figured he'd do better to walk when he had the chance.

What made it worse was that the women were playing their own game of golf on another part of the course—and he was certain Morgan was seething. She was all about equal rights, if nothing else.

As he watched his new buddy Jacob putt at the hole, he

marveled at the afternoon's events. Morgan, correct as always, had led Raquel straight to him. Well, indirectly, of course. Ever since that crazy kiss he and Morgan had shared after breakfast, Raquel had been hanging on his every word. In fact, he was surprised she wasn't here now—but they had a separate women's game, and she'd said she was going to take a nap to prepare for the evening's festivities. He couldn't blame her. Morgan had gone, even after complaining. "Yeah, sounds like great fun whacking a ball into sand pits and trees. I can't wait."

But something tickling the back of his mind kept him from being as thrilled at having Raquel finally, after all these years, interested—and that was thanks to Morgan. Yes, he'd been kind of seeing her in a new light over the past couple of days, but that kiss was supposed to be a throwaway, just for show. For Morgan, it probably hadn't done a thing. And Conor could play along with that, but it had been more than just pretend—and he didn't quite know how to deal with that.

For one thing, he was too old for Morgan. Seven or eight years might not seem like a lot to other people, but he'd always felt like the grouchy old man compared to her free and feisty foul-mouthed ways. Being her boss caused part of that strange dynamic, but the age gap didn't help. As hard as it was to imagine Raquel by his side hanging on his every word, it was that much harder with a gal like Morgan.

And yet, ever since that kiss, the thought kept wafting through his brain like a persistent soft breeze through an open window. It tickled at the edge of his consciousness, enough that he kept turning it over, examining it like he would when helping a new customer figure out the calculation errors in their books.

"Penny for your thoughts," Jacob said as they began walking en masse to the next hole.

No way was he saying a word to his new best friend, a guy he wouldn't talk to again until the next reunion—provided Jacob even remembered him then. "Just coming to grips with why I never pursued golf professionally."

"Yeah, you're no Tiger Woods."

"Takes one to know one."

Jacob chortled, all but admitting he agreed. "So when's the big date?"

Continuing to walk, Conor tried not to frown as he racked his brain to figure out what Jacob was talking about.

God, what a shitty fiancée, even in pretense.

But if he could sound casual, maybe Jacob wouldn't notice the pause. "We haven't set a date yet."

"You're a lucky man, Hammond."

This guy didn't know Morgan—not that she would be a bad wife, but he had his doubts if the two of them would ever be compatible. That was a moot point, though. "How so?" He made sure to stay one step ahead of Jacob so he couldn't see his facial expression, but he was now dangerously close to his two rivals, Bullock and Mills. Jesus.

Jacob started laughing. "Is this a trick question? Lemme just say I'm innocent until proven guilty." He let out an obnoxious chortle, but Conor couldn't even manage to pretend to laugh with him. He was too busy keeping an eye on the other men. "She's gorgeous. And sassy. I love that. She's got a filthy mouth—I bet that's awesome in the sack."

He'd heard enough—even though the guy was right on all counts, and Conor was busy trying to figure out how to keep the employee-boss distance between the two of them. "All right. That's enough."

"But am I right?"

Conor turned. "Enough. That's my fiancée you're talking about there."

Shit. He was even convincing himself. What the hell was happening to him?

CHAPTER ELEVEN

FOR THE STUPIDEST fucking reason, Morgan was excited about the evening's festivities. She could honestly say she'd never participated in a masquerade ball, so this would be a first. Did all high school reunions do weird but fun things like this? And, unlike the other activities, they didn't have to wear their nametags to this event. Maybe the organizers thought they'd rekindled friendships enough now that they didn't need name reminders.

When Conor exited the bathroom wearing the tux he'd rented the day before, Morgan said, "Oh, my God. You looking fucking...*dapper*."

"Dapper? What the hell are you even trying to say, Morgan?"

Giggling, she shook her head. "I mean that in the best way possible, boss. I mean...you look like James Bond or Christian Grey!"

"Who's Christian Grey?"

"Never mind." His bowtie was slightly crooked and she couldn't help herself. She walked across the room and adjusted his tie—only to be assaulted by the scent of his spicy cologne, the one that had been making her mouth water since yesterday when she discovered she might have slightly deeper feelings for this man than she'd originally thought. "Better."

"Thanks." He tugged at one of his sleeves, too, making sure he matched.

Damn...he looked fucking hot, but no way would Morgan ever say that out loud. How the hell would she ever get over this newfound crush?

"You look great, too."

"Like a respectable trophy fiancée, I hope." She wore a sleek white gown with ruffles and sky-high silver pumps, courtesy of Conor's credit card, and her brown hair was piled on her head with tiny wisps framing her face. She'd put on darker makeup as well and wore flashier jewelry than usual. Did Conor even notice?

Probably not. He was newly infatuated with Raquel. And why? Not that Morgan would resent him acting like usual, but the woman was a cast-iron bitch...and Conor didn't seem to notice *that*, either. Or maybe he'd had a crush on Raquel for so long that he didn't care. Or, perhaps, Raquel talked differently to him than—

"Morgan? You okay?"

She'd been pondering a little *too* much, and even though she'd exited the elevator with Conor, she was looking at the ground, walking slowly. "Yeah, I'm fine."

"I think it's down the hall this way and then to the right."

Morgan followed Conor, loving how he took her hand in his to continue their ruse. Sure, it was just an act, but she couldn't help but feel a little thrill about how he held her hand in his, as if he didn't even need to think about it twice.

As if it meant something to him.

Around the corner, there was a big sign on an easel, letting them know that the masquerade ball was just ahead. When they got to a big table, their old friend Kendra stood there, manning the table. "Oh! Conor and...Morgan, right?" With a flair, she placed two checkmarks with a Sharpie next to their names.

"I'm impressed, Kendra."

The woman giggled. "That's my job." Acting serious all of a sudden, she said, "So...ladies to the right and gentlemen to the left. You'll get a mask before you go to the ballroom floor—and, for at least the first hour, we're asking people to leave them on...for fun. After the hour, you can remove them, but we want everyone to mingle and just enjoy yourself dancing behind a disguise."

Morgan wondered what was the purpose of being masked and secretive, but she thought it might be fun. She gave Conor a tiny wave. "See you soon."

He smiled and nodded. At least he appreciated that she was a good sport. When she stepped in the little white room, she was struck by what felt like a lot of catty females. Raquel was there, of course, wearing red. Morgan could swear she felt snotty daggers coming from the woman's eyes—not like she cared. A woman with long brown hair pulled back said, "Ah…let's find you the perfect mask."

The woman had three boxes on a shelf behind the table that she was rifling through. Soon, she turned around, holding a white lacy one. While Morgan wasn't going to complain, she thought she'd be completely washed out with all the white. The mask matched her dress, but it felt like overkill. As she got ready to thank the woman, Raquel approached them. "Hey, Brenda, what do you think?"

God. Morgan had to acknowledge her then. Before she pulled a black mask over her eyes, she said, "Hi, Maureen."

Pasting a sicky sweet smile on her face, she said, "It's Morgan. Good to see you, Dominique."

Morgan could tell the other woman's right eye twitched slightly even under the mask. "White's not exactly your color…but you look nice enough." Then to Brenda, she said, "What about with the mask?"

Brenda told Morgan to go ahead and go through the double doors to the rear before she gave Raquel her full attention. Raquel was the kind of woman Morgan would have loved to go toe to toe with verbally back in school. Now, she just found her obnoxious and exhausting.

The ballroom beyond the doors was already packed with people, more than she'd noticed last night at the cocktail party or this morning at brunch. Hundreds of people. And most of the guys were wearing black-and-white tuxedos just like Conor's. How would she ever locate him?

Then again…this might be fun. There were waiters at the event, too, carrying glasses of wine on their trays. "Would you like some merlot, ma'am?" one asked.

"Of course."

Armed with a glass of red wine, Morgan made her way through the crowd, eyeing the men closest to the doors on the other side of where she'd exited. As she brought the glass to her lips to take a sip, two women were laughing and walking past her but not paying attention, and the one nearest her jostled her elbow as she passed—not even noticing or apologizing for it.

And it would have been okay had she not caused the wine to spill out…all over Morgan's white dress.

Fuck.

Now…Conor might not have been accused in his life of being the most observant guy, but he normally did all right. He would never be on a par with Sherlock Holmes, but that didn't mean he was a complete dolt. For instance, color didn't always register with him, but he was positive Morgan had been wearing white.

And the dress had hugged her every curve. He couldn't have forgotten that.

But the style, the design? No clue. He could only remember that the dress showed a little cleavage. At this point, Conor knew having Morgan play his fiancée had been a bad idea, because he would never be able to look at her the same way again.

As he looked over the ballroom, he realized the problem was that at least ten women were wearing white. Only three of them were near this side of the room, meaning they would have been more likely candidates, unless Morgan had decided to haul ass as soon as she'd left the room with a mask on her face. As the women's door opened again and another woman in white exited, he shook his head. Maybe he'd have to leave it up to his trusty assistant who usually had an answer.

Oh, but this task might not be as difficult as he'd imagined. The woman wearing white who was closest to him had blonde hair, so he could eliminate her immediately—and, if he wasn't mistaken, the person nearest her wearing a white dress was actually male. His build gave him away. Whether he was wearing the dress to be humorous or in all earnestness, Conor didn't know and didn't want to waste time on the question. All he knew was the man wasn't Morgan, either.

But…if he approached a woman in white and it was Morgan, maybe she'd recognize him.

Maybe, though, he should be spending his time looking for Raquel. After all, this was the first time he felt like he might have a real chance.

Had he ever thought this much with his dick before?

The woman in white who'd just left the room was looking

around, so he thought she could definitely be Morgan. She had brown hair—and it had been up, right? This woman's was off her shoulders, piled on her head, not short like the woman next to her, and it didn't look completely like Morgan's hair, but what did he know?

As he approached her, he wondered why the damn music was so loud. They were playing classical music to add to the ambience, but they had it cranked as if they were in a dance club. There were no beats thudding in his chest, but that was only because the sweet music had a soft lilting quality.

"Dance?" he asked the woman in white, ignoring the waiter who approached him with a tray of wine. The woman nodded, and he tried to see through her mask, but the eye slits were too narrow. There was no way to tell if those orbs belonged to Morgan. Conor held out his right hand and she slipped her left in his.

What did Morgan's hands feel like?

Was this woman the right height? The right shape?

He knew immediately that the woman he'd paired with had a poor sense of rhythm, but that didn't mean she wasn't Morgan. That she kept stepping on his toes and not anticipating his next move told him that she'd never danced in this kind of setting before—which could definitely mean it was his employee. He wondered if this woman was trying to control the dancing instead of following his lead, and that could mean his feisty employee as well—although, in fairness, she excelled at taking orders when she needed to.

This gal, though, danced like she had two left feet, or as if she had her left shoe and right mixed up. They weren't compatible dance partners, although Conor mused that she might not make a good dance partner for any man.

The damn song couldn't end soon enough. Dancing had never left him feeling so frustrated before. If this woman *was* Morgan, the first thing he'd do when they got back home was to get her some dancing lessons—on his dime.

When they finished, she curtsied just like a woman hundreds of years ago might have done and then she took a glass of wine from a waiter before disappearing in the crowd. Maybe he and Morgan could laugh about that awkward encounter when riding the plane back home. But it told him one thing for certain—he and Morgan probably had no chemistry, despite his new way of looking at her, a feeling that would fade once they drifted back into the routine.

A woman wearing a silky black dress that ended mid-calf emerged from the women's doors. Her presence wasn't overbearing, but there was no denying her quiet self-assuredness. Conor was drawn to her, but he noticed as he approached that she didn't have blonde hair. Well, he could still dance with her until he could find Raquel or Morgan. At some point, they would unmask, right? Before he could close the gap, a shapely woman in red approached him and took him by the hand. Her blonde hair was twisted at the back of her head, making Conor wonder if it was Raquel—but, at this point, he couldn't wonder anymore. He had to just go with the flow and wait till they could unmask.

This dance was sweet and coordinated, but he still wondered about his first strange encounter. The woman in his arms now was getting pretty close, but her flowery perfume stung his nose and her sharp red nails kept digging into his hands. Those nails might excite him if she were dragging them down his back while screaming his name, but at the moment they annoyed him.

Before she left his arms, she stroked his cheek with her hand before running it down his chest. Then she blew him a kiss through ruby red lips and then sauntered into the crowd. Okay, so maybe that lovely lady had potential. But he didn't have much chance to think about it before a wispy creature in silver whisked him away—and she seemed to be a free spirit, another woman who didn't want to engage in a traditional waltz.

Three dances later, and Conor grew bored. He suffered from what he labelled observation fatigue, his brain unwilling to process any more information to try to ascertain who he was dancing with. He didn't even know if the women he'd led in motion were former classmates or spouses of them, and he'd tired of trying to figure it out.

Then a woman in black moved in front of him and tilted her head to the side, sweetly inviting him to the next dance. She didn't say a word, but he could read her body language just the same. Was this the woman who'd emerged from the doors earlier, catching his attention for some strange reason?

He thought it might be.

Conor held out his hand to take hers, and she rested her soft warm one in his. The brush of her flesh sent a zap of electricity through his body.

Holy shit. Who was this woman?

Unlike all the dances before this, he felt like he could take this woman and win a dance contest with her. She anticipated his every move, following his footsteps, letting him lead her, intuitively moving as one. But there was more to it than that. She wore a spicy scent that, although soft, wafted into his nostrils, adding to the magnetism he began to feel. And, although there was a good centimeter between their bodies, he could feel her heat, her pulse, her aura, and they seemed to meld together.

He had to know who this woman was—and find a way to spend more time with her later this evening.

Ah, the old Conor was back…the *man*, not the unsure teenage kid.

Their dance felt almost like foreplay, even though there was no inappropriate touching—but they were on the same wavelength. When they had to go their separate ways, he'd have to commit something about her to memory so he could identify her sans mask.

But as the music began to fade, he heard a woman's voice on a microphone near the other end of the room. "Ladies and gentlemen," she said as people on the floor stopped moving, "I hope you're enjoying the evening thus far. We'd hoped to add a little fun and mystery to the events tonight, but a few folks felt uneasy not being able to locate their significant others—so it's time to unmask. You don't *have* to if you're feeling a little naughty, but we encourage you to do so."

He could see the woman on the microphone at the back of the room, and she removed her mask as if modeling to the dancing crowd how to do it. Kendra King, the gal who seemed to be running the show, revealed herself to everyone else there—and this was the perfect opportunity for him to discover who the hot woman beside him was…unless, of course, she chose to leave hers on. To encourage her, Conor placed his fingers on the right side of his mask and slowly pulled it up.

The woman in black tilted her head again, but he couldn't read her facial expression. As he pulled the mask off, though, there was no denying the smile crossing her ruby red lips. Coyly, she took a step back, placing a finger on her mask but shaking her head slowly back and forth.

Oh, God, this woman—whoever she was—was a hell of a tease.

He smiled and took a step nearer as she moved back a little as well, as if they were still dancing. That she didn't turn away from him signaled that she wasn't shunning him. She pointed at his face before curling her finger toward herself, inviting him to close the tiny gap, and she tapped the side of her mask.

Was she inviting him to remove it from her eyes?

Conor raised his eyebrows in question as he placed his hands on either side of her disguise. Jesus—this was like Christmas, like he was unwrapping the most mysterious present under the tree, the one that had taunted him for weeks. That wasn't unlike this woman who'd begun taunting him in the space of seconds, inviting him to discover who she was underneath the mask she wore.

He needed to know who she was and, at this point, it didn't matter. He needed to spend more time with this lovely, sexy creature tonight—no matter who she was. The only thing he was certain of now was that she wasn't Raquel.

Peeling off her mask, though, Conor was shocked, because he had never expected to see her face underneath. He'd never had this kind of chemistry with Morgan. What was playing fiancé doing to him?

CHAPTER TWELVE

WHEN MORGAN HAD come back to the party in a new dress (thankful that she had never under-packed for a trip in her life), she'd sought out Conor. In her mind, she'd been sure he would be easy to spot. After all, Conor was tall. But there were a few tall men in the crowd with dark brown hair. The tux he'd rented was a pretty generic black-and-white deal, too.

But when she'd entered the ballroom, she'd looked around, assessing the most likely men and then wandering around a little to try to find out for certain. Taking her best guess, she'd asked this man to dance.

The dance had been sensual, and it had been like they'd dropped their real masks that they wore everyday—the ones that labeled them boss and employee, older man and younger woman, all the reasons they were able to put barriers and distance between them. Dancing with the masquerade disguises allowed them to drop all those conventions and just be themselves, speak with their bodies, and ultimately discover that maybe there was a whole hell of a lot more chemistry there than they'd expected.

Was she going to feel like a complete fucking idiot if this man removed his mask to reveal that he wasn't Conor?

But then she started questioning herself. Was it Jacob, the man who'd seemed to be crushing on her all night, the washed-up quarterback wanting to take another stab at life? He was about Conor's height after all—and he'd wanted to strike up something with Morgan. With the mask and tuxedo in the darkened room, his weird hair might not have been noticeable.

This man didn't seem to be in any hurry to do so, almost like he was frozen, so Morgan reached up to take his mask off herself. She had to know. The man didn't flinch, so she wrapped her fingers around the side of the mask and slowly brought it up, reminding herself that those lips looked like Conor's, the build of his body, the scent of his sandalwood cologne—if this wasn't Conor, she'd be shocked...but, if she hadn't been playing his fiancée, she would have considered spending a little alone time with another man. The only thing stopping her was the loyalty she felt to her friend and boss.

But it was him—his beautiful earth-brown eyes shone as she lifted the mask up over his head, but no smile of recognition crossed his face. Was he angry? Upset? Furious that it was Morgan and not some other woman he'd been hoping to hook up with before they left?

After all the chatter, she led him to remove her mask, too— and she had no idea what he was thinking. The music had started up again and there was lots of talking now, but time all but stood still with Morgan and Conor. She couldn't stand it any longer. "Say something, Conor."

His eyes searched hers as if seeking the answers to ancient unsolved mysteries. His voice was low and angry-sounding, a quality she'd never heard in his words before. "I think we need to get out of here."

She couldn't disagree but wondered the purpose.

Taking her hand, Conor led her through the ballroom and through the men's doors. Morgan stifled a giggle when she saw a couple in the corner making out, as if this were twenty years earlier and their raging hormones had gotten the best of them.

But wasn't that what was happening here with her and Conor?

Well...she knew she'd been finding him more and more attractive as the weekend had progressed, but she'd had a sense that the feeling wasn't mutual. Just because her stupid brain was latching onto the "we're engaged" idea didn't mean Conor's had. In fact, she had the suspicion that he was angry because he felt like he'd been duped by her—that she wasn't the woman he'd expected under the mask, and he was going to give her hell about it.

Maybe she was going to lose her job.

In the elevator, her stomach flipped multiple times as if it were a trapeze artist. There were strong overpowering vibes pulsing off her boss, and for one of the first times ever, she couldn't read him. All she knew was that at this moment, he was not the easygoing, casual guy she'd been working for all these years.

"Conor?"

He shook his head. "We'll talk when we get back to our room."

"There's nobody in here."

Shaking his head again, he kept his face forward, watching the numbers climb as they experienced weightlessness for a moment. That didn't help Morgan's touchy tummy. But when the elevator went *ding*, the doors slid open and Conor grabbed Morgan's hand impatiently, leading her down the hall to their room.

Once inside, Conor asked, "How much did you have to drink tonight?"

What an odd question. "Before some clumsy ass knocked an entire glass of red wine all over my white dress, I had a sip. I didn't have any when I came back. Why?"

She'd seen this look on Conor's face before. When he had a dilemma or a tough customer problem he had to work through, his brows would knit and he'd get a faraway look in his eyes, as if he was digging deep into the caverns of his mind. Why he was doing that now was beyond her.

"I only had a glass."

"So? Are the alcohol police coming to get us?"

Conor didn't give her his usual barely amused grin. Instead, he said, "Was it just me, Morgan?"

"Was *what* just you?"

"What happened back there." She was afraid of admitting the feelings that had been growing for this man. If he wasn't thinking and feeling the same thing, she'd look like an idiot—and things between them would be awkward for a long while.

But he demanded an answer—one she wasn't ready to give, so she countered with another question. "What happened back there?"

He squinted his eyes, scrutinizing her face once more. "I guess it was just me."

Oh, fuck. She was at a crossroads now—and she wanted this man desperately, no matter how afraid she was of telling him the truth. And this wasn't like her at all. Usually, the truth spilled out of her mouth like vomit, and she had no way of stopping it. Why was she now so hesitant?

Conor was loosening his tie, walking across the room to the door.

The real Morgan took over, telling this namby-pamby fearful-in-love girl to step aside. "If you're talking about the strange chemistry between us, it wasn't just you."

Morgan heard the deadbolt click into place before Conor turned, pulling the tie out from his collar. He'd never looked so gorgeous to her before, so appetizing and undeniably hot. She had nothing to lose now. "I can't explain what was happening, but—"

Conor placed his finger on her lips, as if to shush her, but his touch was gentle. Swallowing the saliva that had pooled in her mouth, Morgan tried to figure out if he wanted her to shut up so they could pretend it never happened—or if he had some other motive. His eyes continued studying her face, and she wanted to tell him the answers he was looking for weren't there. There would be no talking, though, because Conor's face was moving closer to hers—and that could mean only one thing.

He definitely felt it the same way she did.

Morgan felt a vice grip her stomach and twist it, sending flurries of moths through her bloodstream. Most people anticipate the first kiss, but Morgan dreaded it. Yes, they'd kissed earlier that day, but it had been bullshit. This would be the real first one. And there was so much emphasis and importance placed upon the first one—how perfect it had to be, how memorable. And she had a list a mile wide of what made a kiss good. The lips couldn't be desert dry, but she didn't like slobbering, either. And passion was important, but the first kiss, while it didn't have to be chaste, shouldn't be a guy's tongue thrust straight down her throat, raping her mouth. She liked finesse, and it was all about timing.

And seeing Conor through his classmates' eyes—the nerd gone good—made her a little skeptical. But it was happening, and there was no stopping it. His mouth approached hers, full speed ahead.

His lower lip gently caressed hers. Ah…a good first step. Then he slowly brought both lips in contact with hers, but there was nothing overbearing about it—it was teasing and playful, exactly what it needed to be. As Morgan's toes curled in her sky-high shoes, she dropped her clutch purse and touched his chest with her hands. The mouth-to-mouth contact with Conor was heady, and so she needed to touch something with her fingertips to help ground herself.

As she parted her lips, Conor took the cue and slid his tongue in. Gone was her anxiety about shitty smooching, replaced by the beauty of the moment. Later on, she would declare the kiss as close to perfection as it could have been.

But she was breathless.

Batting her eyelashes, she tried to bring herself out of the trance she was in. Conor's irises seemed to take over his eyes, making them look even darker than they already were, and the sight of him made her feel tense from head to toe. She was now ready for whatever the evening would bring.

Conor had a freaked out look in his eyes, as if he felt like he'd overstepped his bounds. Before he got any bright ideas, Morgan took matters into her own hands—*literally*. She slid both of them up his chest before winding her right hand around his neck and then splaying her fingers to drive them into his thick, gorgeous brown hair. "Morgan—" She interrupted him by initiating a kiss of her own.

He willingly participated but then said, "Morgan, we can't."

Bullshit. She was ready. This man had passed the kissing test, so she knew he'd probably nail the entire act—and she needed to know now. "Why not? It's not like we work for a corporation that has a fraternization policy. You're not going to fire us for behaving contrary to an employee manual." He frowned and opened his mouth to talk, but she was on a roll. "We're already pretending to be engaged and—"

Conor cut her off again with another kiss.

Another *delicious*, toe-curling, hair-raising, pussy-clenching kiss.

When he finished, he pulled away just enough that Morgan had to open her eyes. "So?"

Conor's face turned up in a lopsided grin. "I can't argue that logic." And then he buried her in another kiss.

This was for real. It was happening. If Morgan allowed herself to stop and think about what was really going on, she would have applied the brakes—because she wasn't kissing just any guy. This was her boss. There would be consequences.

But her flesh was weak…and craving. And Conor kissed like Casanova.

Well, there was no sense prolonging the proceedings. When Morgan was turned on, she didn't need much foreplay, and right now every nerve tuned into the man raising her blood pressure, tightening her every muscle. Morgan moved her hands to his chest again and let her fingers get to work, beginning to work the buttons on his tux where he'd left off after removing his bowtie. Each prolonged, increasingly urgent kiss Conor delivered made her blood swirl that much more, made her need him.

Soon, the shirt was unbuttoned, pulled from his waistband and cummerbund, and she allowed her fingers to play on his bare flesh.

Oh, my God. This is really happening.

As she wound her hands around to his back, determined to figure out how the cummerbund worked, he distracted her by moving his lips down to her neck, pulling the strap off her shoulder. Her muscles grew taut again and she bit her lip as her fingers curled against his back, gripping the cummerbund while avoiding scratching his flesh. But he took over and removed it before she had to keep feeling around futilely.

If any of Conor's classmates had observed the fervor with which they attacked each other and explored one another's bodies, they would have known immediately that they were newly impassioned.

Conor might have been an expert with numbers, but he was no slouch with his tongue, either. Even though they'd had one practice kiss for show before, it couldn't compare to this one. This time, Conor's lips firmly pressed against hers, passionate and desperate. Morgan could feel that through his lips and the way his tongue collided with hers. She didn't want to wait for what would come next, even though the inevitable outcome lay ahead, closer and surer than the sunrise. For a brief moment, she considered putting this off because the timing felt wrong, but she knew if they walked away now, this might never happen. Why? Because, in the back of her mind, she knew this idea sucked—and Conor would agree if she asked him.

Worst. Idea. Ever.

But she didn't care as her fingers tickled his back in exploration. She'd spent all day long seeing Conor through the eyes of Raquel, someone who really didn't care about who him yet who remarked on his incredible sexiness, and it caused Morgan to appreciate that quality. Yes, a long time ago, she'd crushed on him but in the most innocent of ways.

She couldn't help herself anymore. She had to have this man, and it didn't matter that he signed her paychecks. Now, she knew he reciprocated her feelings. What would happen tomorrow made no difference. Morgan's heart and her tingling, begging nerves overruled all those thoughts in her head.

As Conor's lips continued assaulting hers, she moved her hands around to his belly before running them up his chest. Conor held her at the small of her back, letting her focus on feeling his flesh as she began exploring him, returning his kisses with even more fervor than before. His mouth tasted sweet, the remnants of wine lingering, and yet there was a masculine quality to it Morgan couldn't quite identify. Already, she knew she'd find herself addicted to him if she wasn't careful.

Conor's lips broke with hers and he began kissing the side of her neck, so she turned her head to make it easier for him. Pulling down a deep breath through her nostrils, Morgan allowed her fingers to be still while her brain focused on the feel of his lips on her neck. The kiss was warm but soon cooled as he moved farther down, and her nipples grew tight in response, as if those nerves were directly connected to each other.

Finally half in control again, Morgan slid her hands up over his shoulders and then to the sides, pulling his sleeves a little down his upper arms. She wanted the two of them naked, writhing in each other's arms, instead of standing mostly dressed, barely inside the living area of the hotel room. "Take your shirt off, Conor."

When he opened his brown eyes, her breath hitched at how different he looked. The pupils were swollen so much that they were dark and stormy looking, signaling to her that he was as aroused as she, that all kinds of chemicals were flooding his veins, readying him for their imminent joining, turning him into a visceral being that acted on instinct rather than thought.

"Okay, Mo, but you need to take something off, too. This isn't a one-man show." She raised her eyebrows, pondering if a one-man show might be fun to watch. "Who do you think is the boss around here anyway?"

Morgan felt a puff of air exit her lungs in amusement, but when she felt her pussy clench, too, she realized she kind of liked Conor being all take-charge with her. She'd been turned on anyway, but that playful aggression just added to it—especially because he'd never truly been an authoritarian bossy employer anyway. Taking control in the bedroom, particularly when Morgan tended to be pretty headstrong herself, made her knees feel like jelly.

"Yes, sir!" Her tone was playful but her movements were all business. She bent over and removed first one shoe and then the other. As she stood, Conor took her back into his arms—but he pulled the strap off her shoulder before sucking at the flesh there. Meanwhile, his hands were feeling all around her back, almost tickling her.

"Is there a zipper on this thing?"

"No, it's stretchy."

Conor arched an eyebrow and it felt like his eyes were shooting daggers with tips coated in a wicked aphrodisiac. "So I could just peel this thing off you. Is that what you're saying?"

"Pretty much."

Conor took the hint and kissed her hard, pulling up at the sides of her dress until he could slide his hands underneath where he cupped her ass. Holy shit. It was then that Morgan realized she was wet, her panties soaked with desire. But he kept kissing her, not letting her catch her breath, filling her with the sensation that she was barely keeping her head above water, that one wrong move would cause her to drown.

Ah, but what a way to go.

His fingers drifted so damn close to her pussy and it squeezed again, wishing he'd slide a stray digit between her legs just to tease her a little. Curling her toes as if trying to anchor herself to the floor, she dug her nails into his back and took a deep breath, letting his spicy cologne permeate her nostrils. She would forever associate that scent with whatever wound up happening here tonight, that masculine fragrance forever belonging to Conor in her memory hereafter.

Impatient, Morgan was ready to move the proceedings along as well. As much as she was enjoying letting her fingers explore his solid musculature, she wanted to feel his most solid member that was now straining through his slacks, pressing into her lower belly. Moving her hands to his waistband, she felt around for the button holding them together. In seconds, she'd conquered the button before pulling down the zipper. She wasn't quite ready to take his cock in her hands, though, because one last dose of reality flooded her brain.

Oh, my fucking God, Morgan. This is your friend. Your BOSS! What the hell are you doing? Oh, my God, oh, my God, OH, MY GOD!!!

Her conscience screamed at her, but her id tried to tune it out to little avail. *Are we really doing this?* As she started to doubt herself once more, Conor nibbled at her lower lip while squeezing her ass, making her pussy drip even more—causing her rational brain to shut right back off. Logical thinking was not allowed here. As if he could read that part of her mind, Conor began pulling up on her dress. After Morgan helped get her right hand out of the fabric, she figured there was no better time than the present. Once joined again, she fished her hand inside the opening in his slacks.

Holy shit. Not only was he hard…but he was bigger than she'd imagined. No, he wasn't huge like in the trashy novels Morgan liked to read, but he was big enough to fill her up completely.

Like a bolt of lightning, Morgan had a shitty thought as she stroked his cock for the very first time: *what if he's thinking about Raquel while he's doing this to me?* But when he let out a tiny groan, she knew even if that woman had been in his head, she could maybe drive her out, even if just for a little while. She slid her hand down his shaft and then up again, giving a small squeeze to the head, spreading around the drops of precum oozing out of the tip. Her dress still clung to her left arm as he remained paused, as if she had complete control over him, but then he moved again, dropping it to the floor like an unwanted doll.

As if he couldn't get enough of her, his lips met hers in a bruising kiss, one Morgan knew she'd feel later on in the afterglow. But then he pulled away. Leaning over, he took off his shoes and pulled his pants off the rest of the way, but he was looking at Morgan's body, too. Morgan hadn't been a shy adult and she invited his gaze—but her brain, the one she thought had finally shut off, perked up one last time: *Thank God you wore matching underwear.*

Pure white and a little lacier than she usually liked, but they matched.

"You look like an angel, Morgan," he said, his finger touching the lace on the top of the bra on her left breast as he began kissing her neck again. Morgan's eyes closed to enjoy the sensation of his lips as she sucked down a deep breath before he began kissing down toward her cleavage. He pulled down the cup on her left breast, exposing her nipple before taking his tongue to it, flicking and teasing, while his other hand gently squeezed the other one. Her nipple grew hard and Morgan felt like she was going to start panting. Her heart began thudding in her chest, making her feel like she was running a marathon. Instead of panting, though, she let out a long, slow sigh, relishing the way Conor's tongue felt against her rigid pebbly nipple.

Every muscle on Morgan's body tightened, screaming in agony at the torture of prolonged titillation, and she forced her hand up into Conor's hair, grabbing a fistful. "Conor, like any other woman, I love foreplay—but I can't take this anymore. Fuck me already."

Conor looked up from her nipple, once more gazing through dark eyes, but they were now wide, almost as if he couldn't believe she'd said it. "Your wish is my command."

Ha. Finally.

But he wasn't kidding. Yanking her panties half down her thighs until the elastic dug into her legs, he said, "You might want to take those off, because they have no chance of surviving me." Morgan felt a smirk form on her face as she grabbed them and shimmied them down to her knees, feeling the trail of wet juices down her inner thighs, and she let them drop to the floor. Then, holding her about the waist, he lifted her off the ground and pinned her to the wall, kissing her hard once more before impaling her with his rigid cock.

"Holy fuck," Morgan gasped. *He feels amazing.* She hadn't felt like this with Rex, but her pussy fit Conor's cock like a glove, wrapping around him, pulsating to his rhythm. Why the hell was she thinking about Rex at a time like this? Deep down, she knew why, though. Rex had ultimately been disappointing in every way possible.

Moving slowly at first, his cock caressed the walls of her pussy, filling her, stretching her, easing in and out in an almost agonizing way. She could feel her juices flowing faster, his cock growing more slick as he slid back and forth inside her. Letting out a groan, Morgan's thighs clamped around his body, her pussy mirroring the action, squeezing his cock as he continued ramming it inside her.

Then he stopped.

"What the hell are you doing, Conor?" Her voice sounded foreign to her, almost like she was pleading for mercy. Then she growled. "Don't make me beg."

"Trust me." Grabbing her more firmly underneath her ass and thighs, he walked across the room into the bedroom. When he approached the bed, he gently removed his cock from her to lay her on top of the fluffy white comforter. "Sorry. I didn't mean to break the mood, but I wanted us to be a little more comfortable."

Perhaps he'd missed the part where she'd demanded he fuck her? Did he not get the clue that she was tired of waiting?

She opened her mouth to berate him but he licked her nipple unexpectedly, making the words fade from her lips, turning into a quick breath. Arching her back, she shoved the entire top of her breast into his mouth and he suckled and licked and even nipped, forcing another gasp from her throat. Then he traced his tongue up to her collarbone and eased his cock inside her once more, and she wrapped her legs around his torso, as if capturing him.

That goddamned brain of hers made an appearance one last time, asking why the hell Morgan hadn't made sure Conor put on a condom before they'd gotten started. That was fucking dumb, considering she knew he got around. But Conor had always seemed to be super smart when it came to women and keeping his distance, so she prayed he was clean. She knew she was, and she didn't need to worry about pregnancy because she'd been on the pill forever.

She didn't have to push these nagging thoughts out of her head, though, because the way Conor shifted his cock inside her pulled her to the physical. "Shit, that feels amazing."

As if a man possessed, he began driving inside her with such force that her mind focused solely on that part of her body. She could no longer register the sheen of perspiration where their torsos met, nor the sting of his cologne or the fading throbbing in her crushed lips. It was all on his cock and how it had commanded all her attention and adoration. "Oh, God," she moaned. But, after a few minutes, she wondered why she was so close to climax and yet so far away. Her body wasn't letting go, no matter how deeply she breathed nor how she slightly adjusted her pussy to take him in.

"Are you close?" His voice sounded sexy, almost hoarse, and

if she hadn't wanted him before, just that quality would have made her melt.

"I don't know. I thought so but I can't tell anymore." She wouldn't admit it out loud, but she felt almost numb, even though he was giving her the pounding she'd demanded.

Nodding, Conor eased his cock out of her again and Morgan let out a disappointed whine. "Shh." He touched her lips with his finger before tonguing her cleavage, and she sucked it into his mouth. He groaned before removing it from her mouth, taking a nipple in between his thumb and finger as his lips worked their way down her body.

Morgan sucked down a deep breath as Conor spread her legs and, in seconds, his tongue was sliding against her slit. Her pussy clenched again as a cool sensation spread over her body. Her pussy might have been feeling numb, but her clit was on fire and attentive to his touch. "Oh, fuck. Holy fuck. Okay, I can feel that." She could feel his breath against her flesh as he let out a half laugh, but his tongue didn't stop working. Every stroke sent out a crashing wave through her body, amping up her desire, waking up every nerve. Holy shit, she could feel it now. Her thighs began quivering in response.

"Are you close now?"

"Fuck, can't you tell? Don't you dare stop now."

He laughed again and began stroking her in earnest, as if painting a wall with his tongue, but he was swirling his tongue around, and every motion brought her near the brink. Finally, she took another deep breath and an orgasm filled her brain, making her entire world blow up around her. Was she dying now? Because this felt like heaven.

As her moans died down, Conor moved up on the bed and he slid his cock inside her once more. "Are you ready?"

"God, yes."

Conor began pumping and Morgan's orgasm began again. This time, her quivering thighs had something to clamp against, and she felt her pussy massaging his cock with every new wave of delicious ecstasy. "Oh, God, Conor."

In response, he let out his own groan and thrust inside her again with the force of a stallion. He did this not once or twice but three times until he slowed his rhythm, his breathing reduced to panting, as if he'd just run the race of his life. He let out a sigh, and it sounded like sweet music to Morgan's ears.

After a minute of slowing breathing and cooling off, Conor rolled off her, sending another quiver up her spine as he withdrew. The air conditioner felt good against her damp skin but, after another minute, she felt chilly and rolled the side of the comforter over her body. Conor pulled her close, but his eyes were shut and his voice sounded sleepy. "Tell me about that tattoo on your hip, Mo."

Morgan had two tattoos, and their symbolism had become so ingrained in her that she hardly thought of them anymore. One was a super tiny heart on her left wrist, one that most people never noticed because of how small it was—but that one memorialized her grandmother, whom she'd loved dearly her whole life and who'd passed two days before her high school graduation. Her mother—even though she'd just lost a parent—encouraged her daughter to walk for her diploma just the same, because it was "what grandma would have wanted" but also because, she assured her daughter, "grandma would be watching from heaven." Morgan doubted the last sentiment but took to heart just the same that her grandma most certainly wouldn't have wanted Morgan to not walk with her class. She'd held in the tears throughout the ceremony but she took some of her graduation money and, two days later, walked into a tattoo studio that gave her the tiny bit of ink and, when they found out what it was for, gave it to her on the house. Because of that, she returned a month later to get her second one.

"Could you tell what it was?"

Conor raised his torso a little and, seeming to realize he wouldn't be able to see it anyway because Morgan was on her side, lay back down. "It looked kind of like a woman's silhouette upside down, but I didn't get a good look at it."

Morgan considered calling bullshit because he likely got a good look considering he'd been down there not ten minutes ago—but maybe he hadn't been staring at her artwork. "It *is* a woman's silhouette upside down, but she's diving—taking the plunge. When I went to the artist, I asked her to tattoo something that symbolized being fearless. We talked for a little bit and, based on what I said I wanted, the money I had, and her inspiration, this was what I got. And I didn't know what it was until she was done."

"Really?"

"Yeah. I wanted a reminder to be fearless every single day—even with simple stuff, you know? So I was even fearless that day, trusting that she'd find the perfect image for me. And she did."

Conor was quiet for a few moments, stroking her arm with the hand he'd wrapped around her. "That's pretty cool. I'm trying to figure out how to use that against you."

Morgan smiled, knowing Conor would do no such thing and, even if he tried, it wouldn't work. That was the whole point of the tattoo. Her life had changed from that point on and was part of the reason why she'd applied for the job at Conor's business even though she wasn't qualified.

"What about you, boss? What about your tattoo?" Oh, God. Was now really a good time to remind them of their roles? But she sat up and, now that they'd broached the subject, she decided she could scrutinize it without worry. *Build castles in the air.*

"Henry David Thoreau. That's a quote—he says to 'build castles in the air' and not worry about them being there, because they should be, but build 'foundations under them.' I got that tattoo right before I opened my own business."

Morgan, stroking the script letters on his pec, said, "Our tattoos sound similar, don't they?"

"Yeah, actually, they do." Conor yawned then, quietly, but it gave Morgan the urge to do so as well. Afterward, she blinked her watery eyes and rested her head against his chest.

Right now, Morgan would describe her state as blissful, and she refused to analyze it. Instead, she allowed her eyes to drift shut as her mind replayed the evening's events before sleep buried her in a cocoon of sweet nothingness.

CHAPTER THIRTEEN

BECAUSE CONOR HAD awakened at five AM with his body refusing to go back to sleep—thanks to his mind's chatter—he wasted no time heading back to the exercise room in the hotel. Armed with a bottle of water and a lot on his mind, he located the same treadmill he'd used the day before and pounded out a couple of miles and a lot of sweat before his brain came into sharp focus.

Toweled off, he made his way back to their room, surprised that Morgan remained dead to the world. He'd never been able to sleep well in hotel beds on the first night, but he'd been surprised that sleeping on the sofa hadn't been half bad. Last night, though, he'd not only rested in the bed itself, but the slumber had been shitty at best because he kept waking up with a woman next to him. And not just *any* woman, either.

Why the hell had he given into that impulse?

It didn't matter now. What was done was done, but now he wondered what this would do to their working relationship.

Looking back, he marveled at how she'd almost seemed perfect for him—they'd seemed compatible, made for each other. The way she'd responded to his touch, how they'd moved together as if they'd been lovers for years made him think twice about blowing it off as a one-time thing. Unlike his typical conquests, his assistant was someone he cared about.

With Morgan in much the same place she'd been when he'd left, he showered and got ready for the final day of the reunion. Once dressed, he touched Morgan's shoulder and spoke her name, but she mumbled something all but incoherent, telling him she wanted to sleep. He wrote a note and left it on the coffee table in the living room, letting her know he was heading down to the group breakfast, figuring that if she overslept, he could buy her something to eat from the restaurant.

The empty elevator welcomed him, inviting him to relax, but on the next floor, he picked up two occupants—his old pals Bill Bullock and Francis Mills. Both men looked like hell—half-open eyes, sagging cheeks, pinched foreheads. Apparently, these guys had enjoyed the vino a bit too much during the masquerade ball.

That would make them even less pleasant than usual.

But Conor didn't need to be rude. He nodded as they walked on, a somber pair, and then said, "Hey, Bill, Francis." He considered asking them how they were enjoying things so far, but he actually didn't give a shit. After the morning's events, he'd probably never see these two again—or, if he did, it would either be in ten years at the next reunion (if Conor was stupid enough to attend again) or on Facebook. He had no relationship to maintain.

But Bill had other plans. Despite the fact that his face looked like it had served as runway asphalt the night before, his mouth worked just fine. "When are you and your little chickie tying the knot?"

The problem with this ruse was that Conor couldn't remember the lies he'd already told—so he hoped his instincts would guide him right. "We haven't set a date yet."

Francis joined in. "The way the men look at her, I'd already have a ring on that finger, and she'd be barefoot, pregnant, and in the kitchen."

Conor's brain was beginning to struggle with what was real and what wasn't. But whether the engagement was real or not, he knew Morgan well. If she'd been here, she would be tearing into Francis like a tornado. "My fiancée isn't that kind of woman."

"Man, they're *all* that kind of woman—you just have to train them."

Conor shook his head. "Well, you don't know my fiancée. You're talking about her like she's a dog."

Both Bill and Francis cackled, and Conor imagined them as hens on meth, pecking at everything in sight quickly, looking for any vulnerability or anything that would amuse them. These guys hadn't changed in two decades—aside from looking a little older, their brains hadn't grown a bit. There was no evolution to civilized, adult men and they instead behaved in the same stupid middle school way they had up to their senior year. The thought struck Conor, because he knew he himself had changed a lot in the past twenty years and wouldn't trade that growth for anything.

"If it makes you feel better, she's a cute dog."

Inspired, Bill said, "A *bitch*. She's a cute bitch."

Making a lewd face and licking his lips, Francis added, "Hot and tight, yeah?"

Conor felt his ire rise. "If you two don't shut the fuck up right now, I'm going to beat the shit out of both of you. That's my—" Holy shit. He'd almost called her *assistant* without even thinking. "—girlfriend you're talking about."

"Don't get all bent out of shape, man. We're just dickin' with you."

Conor stood his ground but let out a breath. He'd never been a violent kind of guy, but his primal self realized the stakes here if he hadn't responded. That they backed down allowed him to remain civilized. "It's disrespectful and rude and I'd appreciate it if you kept your mouth shut when it comes to my fiancée."

When the elevator stopped, Conor stood his ground, ready to get in a fist fight if that was what it came to. Both Bill and Francis took tentative steps toward the doorway and, when Conor moved aside, nodding, they got off. Francis said, "Sorry, Conor. We were just messing around."

"Just don't let me hear it again." Bill half-heartedly nodded his blond mop of hair and both men began meandering toward the breakfast.

And, instead of following them there, Conor punched a number on the elevator to head back up to his room.

What the hell had Conor been doing all morning? Morgan had heard the door several times, but this last time made her stir completely.

Why the hell was there a little feeling of giddiness inside? She had to knock that shit off right now. No way in hell was she going to carry on with the boss. Last night, they kind of had to. After their sensual dancing, they had to work out the sexual tension they'd both felt—and it had been all her fault, because she'd been toying with the idea this whole damn weekend.

But this was it. No more. Hands off.

The best way to get on with it would be to wash the scent of him off her body, so into the shower she went. As she shampooed her hair and slid the bar of soap over her skin, she remembered all the places Conor had touched her last night and how he'd made her feel.

That orgasm. Damn.

But enough. When she got out of the shower, she was going to return to being her old self.

Wrapped in a robe with her hair up in a towel, Morgan headed into the bedroom to pick out the day's clothing. And there on the couch sat Conor, ruining her perfect plans.

Trying to sound as objective and emotionless as possible, she walked past him into the bedroom while throwing out a simple "Good morning."

But, of course, he followed her and stood in the doorway. "We need to talk."

"Look, Conor," she said, her eyes in the closet as she scanned the three outfits she had left, trying to decide what clothes would match her mood, "I really don't want this shit to be awkward."

"It doesn't have to be."

Inside, Morgan knew she'd made a mistake, but she didn't want to say that to Conor—not now. What if he had deeper feelings for her? And he might. After all, sleeping together hadn't been part of the plan.

But she needed to get him out of her head. She had to break it off; she wasn't quite ready to disappoint him, though. She needed to go jogging now that her body had grown used to it, because she knew that would somehow clear her head. "I'm just not ready to deal with this shit yet. I haven't been up for long. Why don't you go to breakfast without me like you'd planned? And we can talk about it later."

Conor started to say something, then stopped…then started again. "You sure you—?"

"Yeah, I'm sure. I don't want you hanging around waiting for me while I'm busy putting makeup on and stuff." And stupidly jogging *after* the shower. Maybe running could wait—but she still wasn't ready for whatever uncomfortable conversation Conor wanted to have. She needed coffee first—and, before that, she needed to make herself presentable.

Dammit. This whole damn trip had thrown her off her game.

Conor didn't show signs of moving. "Get out of here. I'll be down soon." Frowning, he turned—but he finally left.

She decided ultimately to skip running, but she'd get back on track tomorrow at home. In the meantime, she needed to dress. She didn't give a shit what she wore now because she wouldn't be scrutinized anymore. This was the last day and it would be filled with *goodbyes* and promises to keep in touch and that sort of thing.

That kind of behavior would likely keep the pressure off her—from both Conor and his classmates.

When she entered the big room filled with tables and people half an hour later, she saw that she was a little late. *Oh, what a shame.* There was still plenty of food there, but there was another goddamned slideshow projected on the wall narrated by cute babbling Kendra King, talking about each picture on display. Morgan realized that, while this woman might have come across as a little annoying, one thing was clear—she knew most of her classmates, remembered a lot about their years in school, and seemed to genuinely like them all.

As Morgan glanced around the room, it took her a bit, but she soon found Conor sitting on the left side of the room—and what a surprise. There was Raquel, flirting and carrying on. Well, one thing was for certain. Morgan had been right about how to make the dumb cow interested. Maybe Morgan was too good at her job.

That would have been great if she wasn't falling for her boss. So fucking stupid.

But it would be okay—she'd told Conor not to make a big deal out of it—so she needed to be the same way. If Raquel was snuggled up to Conor, that meant she was interested in him...so mission accomplished. Morgan had already rebuffed Conor, so now she had to get her head straight with *herself.*

Coffee first. If she had coffee, she'd be moving in the right direction. Heading to the beverage table, she grabbed a cup and pushed a spigot, sending a stream of steamy brown liquid into the cup. Just the aroma calmed her distraught mind.

Why the hell was she so freaked out?

And then it hit her. Holy shit. She hadn't written a list—a *real* list—in two days. No wonder she was a fucking wreck. After stirring in creamer and a pinch of sugar, she took a sip of the coffee and then pulled the phone out of her back pocket. As soon as she had her little notes app opened, she began writing a list. Still lame and not realistic, but she was grasping at straws here.

Breakfast – done

Distracted by the slideshow, she sipped more coffee and noticed her phone dimming, so she set the cup down and touched the screen. *Goddammit, Morgan. Focus!* What else did she have to do today?

Board plane

She considered typing *talk to Conor*, but seeing that he seemed to be making strides with Raquel, there was no compelling reason to do it.

Keep playing fiancée

How dumb. God, she couldn't wait to get back to her usual routine, and she was beginning to question if the extra money Conor said he'd pay her was even worth it. After all, she'd considered him a friend before this. Now she was sexually attracted to him but questioning how smart it had been to sleep together.

Kendra's voice over the mike filled the room as Morgan shoved her phone into her back pocket. "This next classmate led the football team to the state championship our senior year." She flashed a picture of a young man in full uniform kneeling on the grass of the football field, holding the pigskin in the cradle of his arm, glaring at the camera. Morgan had seen a million pictures like it when she'd gone to school. That face she recognized as...

Jacob. And behind her, she heard him say, "That's me."

Turning slightly to the right, Morgan saw that he was talking to her. "Yes, I could tell. You were definitely into the moment, weren't you?"

He chuckled, his blue eyes lighting up. "Yeah, those pictures were a big deal."

Like a ton of bricks, Morgan grabbed onto a great idea. If she spent her breakfast flirting with Jacob, even knowing it would go nowhere, she'd soon forget last night's impropriety.

"So what do you do now, Jacob?" Was this guy her type? Hell, no…but she could easily pass the time yakking at him for half a day. When she and Conor got back home, she wouldn't think twice about this man—but she'd hopefully be over her boss, too.

"Right now, I work for the gold mine up the hill." He pointed behind him, as if Morgan knew what the landscape looked like outside. "Been there for about four years."

All Morgan could think about was what she knew about how mines destroyed the environment—but that kind of talk wouldn't be very friendly or cozy. "Do you like it?"

"It has its moments, you know. I've had jobs I like better, but I've had lots worse, too. They treat us good there, so that's all that matters, right?" She nodded, grabbing a small plate she could throw some pineapple chunks on. As she did that, she noticed a woman with pinched lips painted in mauve giving them the evil eye.

Morgan leaned over and whispered in Jacob's ear, something she knew would endear him to her. "I think that lady over there wants us to lower our voices."

Jacob leaned to the right a little so he could see the woman in question, and he pointed with his head. "The woman with brown hair pulled back? The one in purple?" Morgan nodded. "Don't worry about her. Her name's Diane and she was even a fuddy-duddy back in the day. Probably a librarian today, shushing people all day long. If she doesn't like it, she can move closer to ol' Kendra."

Morgan thought the woman might have been able to hear that remark, so she said, her voice low, "Why don't we go sit back there?"

"The table way over there with nobody else?"

"Yeah—unless you don't want to."

"Works for me. What can I carry for you?"

Maybe Morgan could enjoy this for the duration, even if she didn't really need his help. "I think I've got it." When they got near the table, though, Jacob pulled a chair out for her. "Thank you."

"My pleasure." Had Conor even pulled out a chair for her over this weekend? Probably not.

As Kendra continued talking about classmates' accomplishments during their senior year, Morgan said, "Shit. How big was your class anyway?"

Jacob shrugged. "I dunno. Kendra could probably tell you how many kids graduated and how many dropped out, but I couldn't even guess. Seemed like a lot at graduation, like it was never gonna end."

"That's because graduations are boring."

"You got that right." Jacob finished off his Red Bull before he asked, "So how long you and my man Conor been dating?"

Oh, now Conor was his man? Like they'd been best friends in high school who'd never lost touch? And Morgan knew that telling lies could get her in huge trouble, because she wouldn't remember what she'd said if asked again...but her answer would work. "Oh, a while." Her reciprocal question was downright silly—yet she said it with a straight face. "What about you and Raquel?"

He laughed. "Believe it or not, I have not tapped that." Ugh. She should've known a guy like that would use that damned expression. "We were prom king and queen, and two nights before the dance, she'd broken up with her boyfriend and made out with me at a party, but she was back with him by the time they crowned us. I guarantee if she hadn't been dating the quarterback from two years earlier, she would have been my girl."

Aw, poor guy. "So why don't you ask her out now?"

Jacob shook his head, peering into his mug. "Nope. No way. I enjoyed catching up with her, but she's a train wreck, Morgan. And no way could I afford the things she likes. I think that's why she's latched onto your boy. It's been no secret since our last reunion that he's got lots of money." He glanced at the front of the room, where Raquel was rapt in the slideshow...but that didn't stop her hand from possessively holding Conor's arm. In a way, Morgan was glad they'd been so successful at their secondary mission, and she wondered if she was jealous merely because he was now someone she couldn't have.

Fucking stupid.

"Doesn't that piss you off?"

Morgan's fork paused in mid air. "What?"

Jacob chin-nodded toward Conor's table. "The way Raquel's sunk her claws in him."

How would she act if she were truly engaged to her boss?

Honestly...she'd be over there, telling Raquel to hit the road—and she'd probably call her a couple of crass names while she was at it. But she was doing exactly what her boss had paid her to do, meaning she couldn't complain out loud. So she raised an eyebrow. "Who's leaving with him tonight?"

His nod seemed wistful, as if understanding that meant he had no chance with Morgan. But he wasn't about to give up. "Someone might want to tell that to her."

The nervy woman had her lips to Conor's ear—and Morgan had to bury the jealous bile frothing in her gut. She smiled sweetly as if nothing was wrong, but inside a volcano brewed, ready to erupt.

CHAPTER FOURTEEN

CONOR WAS TORN. He had never, in all his thirty-something years, been presented with a dilemma like this. Yes, as he'd grown older and he'd had many a lady friend, but he'd never had two women vying over him.

Of course, he had to remind himself, it was all a ruse. Morgan wasn't *really* fighting for him, even though they'd consummated their fake engagement in style last night. Why the hell couldn't he get Morgan's smooth flesh and responsive moans out of his head?

Last night was nothing.

So, instead of relishing the feeling of being fought over, he needed to focus on what was real—and that reality was equally amazing. Raquel Bettis—*the* most sought-after girl in high school—was giving *him* all her attention. It was true that he hadn't wanted this kind of attention before he'd come, but he hadn't expected the queen of all the former high school beauties to be fawning all over him. She was worthy of rule breaking.

They'd finally stopped whispering to pay attention to Kendra's sweet but boring slide show, and Raquel had rested her hand on his forearm minutes ago. Now she was stroking it slowly but paying attention to the pictures in front of them, and Conor allowed himself to wax nostalgic. He could remember as a young nerd attending some of the football games and watching Raquel, her hair pulled up in a tight ponytail, while she performed those amazing kicks that nearly hit her head—splits in the air—before bouncing and clapping, and then the cheerleaders would begin another routine. She'd never looked at him once when he'd sat in that crowd, but he'd leered at her, stalker-like, averting his gaze to the game whenever the crowd went wild.

She hadn't changed much. As he looked at the screen while Kendra continued showing pictures of big events that had occurred during their senior year, Conor tried to conjure up how Raquel looked right now without turning to stare…but his brain kept flashing pictures of Morgan: Morgan in the elegant black lace dress he'd helped her remove last night—and, naturally, then his brain saw her beautiful breasts, smooth tummy, and—

"Do you remember that? Oh, my God, that was so much fun!"

Conor glanced to his right, looking in Raquel's blue eyes, trying to register what he'd missed with his daydreaming. He tentatively nodded and gave a smile before looking back at the slideshow, which displayed pictures of a bonfire. None of the bodies surrounding the fire were recognizable because huge flames dominated the pictures.

"Why don't you ever come to homecoming, Conor?"

"I'm too busy working. Why? Do you attend every fall?"

"No…not *every* year…but I do like to go when I can."

Conor didn't say anything, but he imagined Raquel got a vicarious thrill from attending homecoming, reliving her old glory days. Conor hadn't hated high school, but he hadn't been one of the top dogs. It wasn't till he'd left that life had really begun. If he and Raquel hooked up, he'd have to show her just how good life could be in the here and now instead of living in the past.

Her eyes were once again glued to the front of the room, eager to take in the next photo Kendra displayed, while most of her audience fell into a stupor, bored by the never-ending virtual yearbook. As she showed photos from a fall choir concert, Conor struggled to find some common ground between him and this woman he'd long thought of as ideal. Ordering his brain to focus on her and not on last night's dalliance with Morgan, though, was easier said than done.

Last night was a mistake, though. Morgan was his assistant, and it would be near impossible to maintain a professional relationship if he was busy banging her—or thinking about it constantly. In fact, he doubted he'd be as productive if he had a girlfriend nearby. He'd crossed a line last night, and he needed to figure out how to correct the wayward path he'd led them on. His dick had a difficult time thinking that way, though.

Photos of the football team winning the state championship flashed in front of them, and Conor wondered where the hell Morgan was anyway. She'd told him she would come to breakfast soon, but she hadn't yet shown up. It didn't take much effort to pry his eyes away from the Christmas concert to turn so he could look through the crowd. The lights in the room were on but dim, and he saw the signs of too much drinking on many a classmate's face. Tired, droopy, bloodshot eyes and sagging, lined expressions gave their indiscretions away. Morgan should have stood out like a sore thumb—youthful, vibrant, a devilish grin like always—but he wasn't seeing her. His eyes wandered to the buffet where a couple of folks were scraping up seconds, and it wasn't until he looked to the left, close to the very back of the room, that he saw Morgan at a nearly empty table.

Empty except for Jacob Martin, star quarterback—the guy who'd been credited all these years for taking state. And the two were deep in conversation, oblivious to everyone around them, as if no one else existed.

If sleeping with her had been a mistake, why the hell was a furious beast rumbling in his chest?

After watching Raquel paw Conor's arm like he was a scratching post, Morgan reminded herself something she'd learned years ago: the best way to get over a guy was by having sex with someone else.

Yes, sex. Not just dating but knee-knocking, animalistic, filthy, dirty, wicked sex.

She'd analyzed it, because she wasn't a one-night stand kind of gal. In fact, for years, she'd had a friend with benefits (until he'd gone and gotten in a super-serious relationship; now he was married with baby number one on the way). He'd been her go-to guy to take her mind off a bad relationship and she always did the same for him, but when he was no longer available, she did what she had to do. Now...the forget-another-guy sex didn't even have to be amazing, but it gave her warped mind something else to think about, her emotions something else to fixate on.

Jacob had zeroed in on her, shown interest, so why the hell not? Yeah, his hairstyle hadn't evolved with the times, but his blue eyes hadn't aged a day and he had a hell of a captivating smile and smooth-as-mocha voice. Finishing her coffee, she scooted her chair closer and Jacob didn't object. Morgan had no plans to copy Raquel, but the woman had the right idea. A touch, subtle or otherwise, would communicate interest. So she placed her hand on his wrist and asked, "Did you play college football?"

Jacob's eyes lit up but he frowned. "One year. I couldn't keep my grades up, though. Plus I wasn't going to a school that seemed to get the attention of the NFL, so I figured that was just a pipe dream. Played some community football a few years, but it's not the same, you know? Having someone pull a flag off me isn't the same as absorbing their tackle."

Morgan raised an eyebrow. "Oh, you like it rough, do you?"

Cocking his head, his blue eyes seemed like oceans in a desert, and she saw in them recognition. "You saying you'd like to play touch football with me sometime?"

Grinning, she nodded. "I think that would be fun." She got ready to add that she was considering doing it right that moment when she was interrupted.

"Ah, I wondered where you were, honey." Morgan pulled herself from Jacob's eyes, but she recognized Conor's voice long before she looked at him. His foreign expression left her feeling bewildered. What was going on with him? Last she'd looked over, he was enjoying basking in goddess Raquel's presence.

Instinctively, Morgan pulled her hand off Jacob's wrist as if the man was a hot stove burner—as if she were truly engaged to her boss. And if they were already lying, what would one more hurt? "I couldn't find you when I got here, and Jacob offered to keep me company while I ate."

"It didn't look like you were eating."

Jacob said, "Nothing happened, man."

"*You* stay out of this, quarterback!"

Now a few tables around them turned to see the show, considering the boring one at the front, now highlighting the dance on Valentine's Day, was failing to keep their attention.

Conor continued, "This is between me and my fiancée."

Morgan wasn't the type to get embarrassed, especially among strangers she didn't know and would never see again, but poor

Jacob looked like he was about to die. Taking two steps, she grabbed Conor's arm. "Let's talk about this in the hall."

"No. We're going to deal with this here."

"*I'm* not, and you can't fuckin' make me." Furious, she marched out of the huge dining room and into the spacious but quiet hall. She hoped they hadn't made too big a commotion so that Kendra could make it to graduation without losing her entire audience. Standing in the carpeted corridor with her hands on her hips, ready to verbally spar, she expected Conor to march through the door. Technically, he *could* try to demand that she do what he'd asked as her boss, but he'd crossed the unprofessional line a while ago. He couldn't play the employer card right now.

But through the door came Jacob. Sweet, earnest, and sincere, he asked, "Does Conor beat you?"

It took a few moments for Morgan to register what Jacob was saying—and then she burst into laughter. "Oh, Jacob, that's so sweet. But no. Conor's not abusive."

"Are you sure?"

"Yes." And, as if on cue, Conor marched through the doors, his nostrils flaring like a bull. "He can be an asshole at times," she said, looking straight at her boss, "but he's never laid a finger on me."

Conor seemed a bit calmer, but Morgan couldn't tell where his irises ended and his brown eyes began. "Excuse me, Jacob, but could I have a few moments alone with my fiancée?"

Jacob clenched his jaw before he told Morgan, "I can stay here if you want."

"Thanks, Jacob…but I think I can take care of myself."

Reluctantly, he took two steps back. "I'll be right behind those doors if you need me."

Morgan nodded. "Thank you." She could feel the anger rippling off Conor in waves, adding fuel to her own fury. As soon as the doors closed behind Jacob, she hissed, "What's your fucking damage, Conor?"

"I might ask the same thing, Morgan. What are you thinking? If you're supposed to be my fiancée, you shouldn't be flirting with one of the guys here."

"And just what exactly were you doing with Raquel?"

"Here's the deal. She wasn't doing anything so inappropriate—or out of character—that my former classmates would question it. What *you* were doing looked pretty out of line."

Wow. "Really? *You're* completely out of line, Conor. You made a big fucking deal back there. What would have looked innocent now appears highly suspect. And that's on you," she said, poking his chest with her finger. "It's unprofessional."

"Unprofessional?" Conor scoffed, a look of surprise on his face. "No, *last night* was unprofessional."

What the fuck was he saying? Morgan couldn't stand it anymore. Was he accusing her of seducing him? And just what had gotten into him anyway? Unable to stop herself, she slapped his face. "Finish this fucking façade on your own. I'm outta here."

Conor watched Morgan stomp down the hall. Shaking his head, he couldn't help but notice how those jeans hugged her ass, the breezy sleeveless pink shirt merely highlighting her shape. He could still feel the sting of her hand on his cheek, and he supposed he deserved it. Had he gone too far?

And why the hell was he jealous? Of Jacob Martin, no less? The guy, though nice enough, would just as soon be back in his high school quarterback uniform, calling plays both on and off the field. Now that he was no longer leader of the pack, he seemed rudderless. And that had been twenty years ago. Poor guy. Conor didn't doubt Jacob would do well with a good woman in his life, but Morgan needed someone more her style, more her speed.

Conor might not have been that man, either, but he was a damn sight closer than Jacob. And he cared about her—on the inside as well as the outside, probably more for her mind and soul than her body.

And even if she didn't want a relationship with him—which was probably the case—he needed to apologize for going too far. Even if he had just been worried about what he saw, Morgan was a grown woman, capable of making her own decisions—even if she was technically on the clock.

Don't be stupid. Of course, she doesn't want any man here, even you. You're all at least eight years older...

So instead of standing there acting helpless, Conor knew he needed to take action. Morgan likely went to their room, so that was where he was going to go.

But he heard the doors behind him open again, and he half expected the presentation to be over, sending people flooding into the halls, grateful to be relieved of the boredom. When he turned, though, he found the hall empty except for tall, lithe Raquel, blonde hair flowing, azure eyes shining, taut body making a beeline for him.

Maybe the best way past the ridiculous emotions he was overwhelmed with would be to give into this little thing—a trophy girl from eons ago, one who'd been unobtainable back in the day...and now she actually wanted *him*. She wasn't gunning for Jacob Martin, star quarterback, or any of the other athletes who'd swarmed their school back in the day.

The way she sashayed down the hall toward him confirmed it: she wanted *him*. Just that knowledge empowered him, made him realize he could slay dragons or face a posse for her. If this woman needed rescuing, he would do it.

"Are you all right, Conor?" she asked, closing the gap and once more touching his arm.

Yeah, this felt right.

"I'm fine."

"Why don't we get out of here?"

A grin turned up the corner of his lips. "What do you have in mind?"

She flashed a seductive smile at him before sliding her arm through his to lead him down the hall, arms linked as if taking a romantic but chaste stroll. "Just follow me."

Raquel paused at the elevator and pressed the up button. Just then, a few people started to trickle out of the dining room, finally relieved by Kendra. The elevator doors opened and Raquel pulled on Conor's arm before she pressed the button for the fourth floor. Conor knew there would be a crowd joining them, so he took his arm out of Raquel's. It didn't matter what they might be doing—he didn't want to give the impression that he was going to cheat on his supposed fiancée. And he shouldn't feel guilty. They weren't actually engaged, and it didn't matter that Raquel didn't know.

He'd probably confess that to her at some point.

But Raquel leaned over and stabbed the button that closed the doors. Apparently, she wasn't interested in sharing the space with others. "We're going to my room, Conor. I don't know how Maureen would feel about that."

"*Morgan.*"

"Right."

"We're not married yet." Why the hell did he feel like a complete ass saying what was on his mind?

"*Oh.* Well, that sounds like fun to me." When the doors opened, Conor held out his arm to allow Raquel to go first. As soon as he stepped out, she took his arm again as if she owned him. "A lot of men will fuck a stripper at their bachelor party for the same reason. Last chance to taste a little foreign pussy before settling down to the homegrown boring, you know?"

He'd had no idea Raquel had such a filthy mouth...but something deep in his loins liked it. His blood was swirling, his curiosity piqued. He wondered what Morgan was doing right now, if she'd tracked down Jacob and was doing the same thing. It didn't matter. The only way to get naked Morgan out of his head was to drown out that memory with a new one—and Raquel seemed to sense just what he'd need.

Raquel slid the card in the slot, her long red nails pulling it back out when the tiny light blinked green. What would those claws feel like on his back as he drove into her over and over? As he followed her into the room, his eyes took her in from head to toe. Her body looked just like it had back in the day: tall, limber, but her breasts were bigger, fuller—ripe and juicy—and he wanted to taste them first. Her hair was longer than it had been back then, but it was more beautiful, flowing like a mane, and the violet dress she wore hugged her every curve, telling Conor she was proud of her assets.

When she turned after tossing her purse on the desk, she took his hands in hers, pulling him farther inside the room. "I hardly remember you from school, Conor, but what a man you've turned out to be." She snuggled up to him then, close enough to press her breasts into his torso, and Conor let go of all the extraneous thoughts flying through his head. "You smell like success," she said as she stretched up to kiss him.

Had he misheard what she'd said? "What?"

"You smell delicious." Then, wrapping a hand around his neck, grazing the flesh with her talons, she pulled his head down to hers. She pressed his lips into her full, pink ones and a surge of chemicals dumped into Conor's bloodstream, preparing him for the mating ritual. Her lips were soft and felt almost right—but her tongue fought with his, tasted foreign, not like what he'd been expecting, her musky perfume clashing with the spicy smells he'd anticipated.

But he would power through it.

As he adjusted to her kisses, he began exploring her back with his hands. Yes, her body was firm, curvy, and well-maintained—but it wasn't the body he'd wanted to run his hands over.

This wasn't right.

But Raquel ended the kiss and stepped back enough, pulling her skin-tight dress up and then over her head. Oh, there was no doubt she was a gorgeous woman…and Conor would be a fool not to take what she was offering. So when she sauntered up to him in nothing but white panties, bra, and heels, he took her in his arms and kissed her like there was no tomorrow.

CHAPTER FIFTEEN

CONOR HAMMOND WAS was a scum-sucking asshole.

Seriously. How had she never seen it before? Maybe working together—yet rarely socializing with one another—had something to do with it. When you had to be professional and put on your best self or else risk losing customers (and an employee), maybe you avoided being the jerk you were at the core.

That had to be it.

But, as she forced herself to not shove clothes in the suitcase, instead folding them so they wouldn't wrinkle, no matter how her anger urged her to throw caution to the wind, she tried to figure out another reason for his behavior. How could he even dare to accuse her of doing the same thing he'd been doing, and all after having a highly unprofessional romp in the hay the night before?

After seeming to be the smartest guy she knew, Conor now appeared to be one of the dumbest. Fuming, she tried to push all those thoughts out of her mind, focusing merely on packing up everything so she could make a clean getaway. Without even looking it up, she knew she had enough money on her credit card to rent a cab to get to the airport—although it *was* in the next town. At least, she *thought* she had enough.

She owned the rash decision. The fallout could be dealt with later.

She went to the bathroom to gather up her makeup and other toiletries when she heard the main door open. "I'm sorry. I don't need housekeeping right now," she said as she exited the bathroom, cradling all manner of things in her arms.

But it wasn't housekeeping.

It was Conor.

"What do you want?"

"What are you doing, Morgan?"

"What does it look like? I'm leaving."

"Hey, I wanted to apologize...tell you I'm sorry. I didn't mean to upset you."

"Well...you did a pretty good job for not intending it."

She could see confusion in Conor's chestnut eyes. "Don't go."

"Why not? I think you already got what you wanted at this damned reunion—deflecting the women you didn't want but snagging the one you did...so you really don't need me anymore." She stormed in the bedroom and dropped the contents of her arms into the open suitcase on the bed.

"No, not really." He followed her, getting close enough to touch her upper arm with his hand. "Raquel...I might have *thought* I wanted her, but I don't. And spending time with her confirmed that. So thank you for helping me figure it out."

Morgan grimaced but couldn't compel her body to back away from him. She could figuratively stab him, though. "That's what you paid me to do. But I didn't help you figure it out anyway."

"Yes, you did, even if you don't realize it."

She bristled at the thought of helping him with his woman problems now, and that helped her pull away and begin marching back to the bathroom to gather up what was left.

"Morgan, would you stop?"

"I'm busy, Conor. Leave me alone."

"Dammit, woman, you're so stubborn." Morgan snorted while walking over to the shower, double checking that she'd gotten everything out of there. When she turned, Conor was right in front of her. "Tell me you didn't feel anything last night."

Was he really going to bring up that up? Something that should be buried ancient history, never to be spoken of again? Seriously...thinking about it ruined everything. "It doesn't matter what I felt."

"It *does*, Morgan. I know you want to pretend it didn't happen, but it *did*."

She swallowed, unable to deny the look in his eyes. Not only did he not want to pretend last night didn't happen, she knew he was remembering the details. And when Conor's eyes got dark like they were now, like they'd been last night, she found herself wanting nothing more than to feel him inside her once again.

But that was dangerous—because if she thought she felt something for him now, a second time would make it lots worse.

She took a step back until her shoe hit the tub, making it impossible to put any significant distance between them. "Okay, but that doesn't mean we have to analyze the shit out of it, Conor. What's done is done."

One step closer and all she could feel was the heat between their bodies, palpable, alive. "It's not that simple, and you know it. It might be done, but it lingers..."

Morgan swallowed, looking up into those captivating umber orbs. This time, as his face approached hers, she wasn't pushing him away. As he gazed in her eyes, he brought his hand to her face and, cupping her jaw, brushed his thumb against her lower lip. She couldn't help the automatic response of her body, begging him to touch her in more places, and she closed her eyes—whether to try to block out the emotions or invite them in, she didn't know. But by the time his lips touched hers, she grabbed the front of his shirt to pull him firmly against her.

She couldn't deny her baser feelings any longer.

And she decided that, if she was going to allow this to happen, she was going to own it—take charge, even. So she wrapped one hand around the nape of his neck and met his tongue with hers with force.

God, he tasted so good. How had she forgotten the flavor of his mouth already? It could so easily become her heroine.

As the kiss intensified, Morgan felt her nipples grow rigid as her breathing deepened. Holy fuck. Conor Hammond most definitely was an asshole—but he was amazing in bed and impossible to resist...and she wasn't going to deny herself one last roll in the hay.

Conor could feel in the tightness of her muscles that Morgan was trying to resist him but failing miserably. If she pushed him away or cut him off or even just said no, he'd walk away, no questions asked. He'd have balls as blue as the Colorado sky, but he'd back off just the same.

Fortunately, his instincts were spot on. Morgan was responding to his touch like a wilting flower sucks up water. She might have told him none of what happened before mattered, but she was lying to herself if she really thought that. They now had a history and even if her logical mind wanted nothing to do with him, her body remembered.

His did, too.

He kissed down the side of her neck and he could hear how the quality of her breathing changed in response. No longer steady, the air travelling to her lungs sounded slight and jagged— and his body reacted to it, letting the first surge of blood charge below his belt in anticipation of what was to come.

The way her nails dug into his neck only fueled the fire.

He continued tasting the sweet flesh of her neck, licking and kissing until he got to the front of her throat. Once there, Morgan shoved her fingers into the hair on the back of his head, seeming to demand that he kiss her on the lips again, and he obliged. But then he sucked on her lower lip while running his tongue along that sensitive area in his mouth, as if savoring a lollipop.

His cock began to throb, and there was no stopping it. Hard as he tried, he couldn't make it stop. Morgan might have thought this behavior was thanks to Raquel, but that woman, even with the small nostalgic attraction he felt for her, couldn't have elicited this response. His cock was hard for Morgan, and it wouldn't be satiated until he felt her walls closing in on him once more.

But he wasn't going to start removing her clothes—yet. He needed her to give him a signal first, like taking them off herself. It would be the only way he'd know for certain that he wasn't coercing her or making her do something she truly didn't want to.

And he got his first sign shortly after that, when her hands worked their way up underneath his t-shirt. Her fingers were warm but they felt tingly against his skin, as if she were a live wire sending arcs of electricity into his flesh, sending more blood diving down his body, making his head feel almost airy. His heart was pumping harder now, his breathing deeper, his muscles tight, ready for the ultimate release.

As her hands made their way up his belly, he decided it was time to get her undressed, too. His fingers grasped her first button and pulled it through the hole and he left her lips still wanting more so he could kiss her at the divot where her throat met her body, the little hollow that seemed vulnerable but sexy and irresistible to him. And the way her breathing changed again at the touch of his lips further aroused him more than any aphrodisiac might. His fingers continued working their way down her blouse, undoing one button at a time while he felt her hands move to his back, still underneath his shirt.

Once he had her blouse completely open, he kissed at her cleavage, wanting to run his tongue over every square inch of her beautiful body—but before he could begin, she yanked on his shirt from the back, demanding that he pull it up over his head. He grabbed it at the front to help her get it off and, as he pulled it off his arms, her lips attacked his chest. She took his nipple in her lips and sucked on it before swirling her tongue all around. Conor never would have guessed what a turn on that would be or that the area was even sensitive. He'd had women tongue his taint and asshole, between his toes, suck on his fingers, lick behind his ears—and it was all good—but this was something new yet simple.

And fucking amazing.

If he'd thought the blood was stampeding toward his cock before, he'd had no idea. He could now hear his heartbeat in his ears, and the rhythm was quickening.

In the meantime, that lacy little red bra Morgan hid her breasts behind was taunting him, so while she licked his nipple, sending hints of ecstasy to come through his nerves, he forced his hands to respond to his brain's command, and he slid them up her back until he encountered her bra strap below her shoulder blades.

Damn it. There were no clasps back there.

Which meant it must hook in front.

That was okay, because he glided his hands around, letting first his palms brush over her nipples, pebbly even through the fabric, and then he turned his hands so that his fingers met in the middle to work the two sides apart.

While he undid the clasp, Morgan's fingernails grazed the flesh of his abs, sending a fresh wave of chemicals through his body, making his head feel light again. His breath caught then, as if stopped by a physical force, and his cock throbbed, letting him know his body was on fire, fully primed—not that he'd needed much coercion.

Morgan, on the other hand, might need more from him—and he was more than happy to oblige. The clasp undone, he pushed the cup holding her left breast aside, taking her nipple in his mouth, savoring both the flavor and firmness of her sensitive flesh. While his tongue worked, his hand removed the opposite cup and his thumb found the other hardened areola and gave it the attention it craved. Meanwhile, Morgan's fingers were unbuttoning his jeans, keeping his mind preoccupied and distracted, making it more difficult to focus on her needs.

The last rational thought he experienced was hoping to hell she didn't mind that they were nowhere near a bed—because he was going to fuck her right here and in short order.

If she was ready, of course—and there was one sure way to tell.

Conor met her lips again, hoping to get her to pause in her relentless pursuit of his cock. Oh, he wanted her touching him there, but he had a mission to complete first, and that was to discover if her pussy really wanted him inside her. So he kissed her firmly and she responded, the motion of her fingers slowing as his sped up, unfastening her jeans, pulling down the zipper, and then entering inside. He fingered the lacy top of her panties, and his cock throbbed once more, eager to plunge deep inside her. It was all but inaudible, but his heightened senses heard the slight gasp, felt how her fingers clenched around the sides of his jeans as if she needed something, anything, to hold onto.

Working his way inside her pants, he slid his fingers over the top of her panties. The space restricted movement, but as his middle finger rubbed over the silky fabric, he couldn't mistake the slick wetness that had soaked completely through. Knowing she was as turned on by him as he was her was the height of arousal, and his kiss grew harder, mirroring how his cock wanted to ram into her pussy, sending waves of pleasure throughout both their bodies.

Sliding his finger back with the intent of leaving that tight space in order to pull her jeans off, he rethought his stance as she breathed a soft moan, the sound of her voice like a caress on his eardrum. Instead of pounding into her immediately, he could bring her even closer to the brink of orgasm now. So he moved his finger side to side over the hard nub, hoping to increase her pleasure and excitement.

That her breathing changed to deep gulps from tiny desperate pants told him he was working his magic. She let out another groan and he buried his head in her neck to give his mouth something to do, to help him remain patient while he helped increase her arousal. But as he continued to stroke her, she removed her hands from his chest and grabbed the sides of her jeans to shimmy them down past her hips, and he suddenly had more room to maneuver.

This was turning out to be easier than he'd expected.

Even though there was more space for his hand, Conor didn't want to move his finger from outside to inside her panties for fear of breaking whatever spell they'd cast. Morgan was on the verge of climax and he was getting pretty damned close, too, so he decided to just keep doing what he was doing. She'd responded well to a similar technique yesterday, so why not do that again?

"Mmm." God, he could listen to the sound of her voice all day. That purr alone was a hell of a turn on. While all her muscles felt taut, her voice sounded like jelly, like she was melting into his hands. So he kept swirling that finger, increasing the pressure and speed just slightly until her breathing picked up tempo.

All but scrambling, Morgan grabbed her jeans and panties and pulled them down farther, and the way she bent made it impossible for Conor to keep his finger in place. After a second, he realized she was getting ready to join, so he followed suit, pulling his jeans down his legs. Before he could pull them completely off, though, Morgan had hers off one foot and demanded his complete attention. Grabbing his jaw, she kissed him hard on the mouth. He knew what she needed, even though she didn't say a word. Too desperate to seek out a soft piece of furniture, he wrapped his arms around her just to lift her up on the counter—which put her at the perfect level.

They hadn't used a condom the day before, hadn't even thought to, so he knew he'd be okay without it now. Consuming her mouth once more, he slid her forward on the counter and she wrapped her legs around him, ready to take in his entire length.

As his cock found its way inside her, Conor allowed the sensations to overwhelm him. Every nerve stood at attention as her soft cave massaged his entire cock, already delivering an overload of pleasure. There was no need for him to hurry now, no reason to rush through the process, because the end was imminent.

He doubted, at this point, if even an earthquake or a fire could stop what was coming.

Morgan's kiss grew distracted as she seemed to focus on her body, and tiny noises began spilling from her mouth, so Conor wanted to concentrate on giving her what she needed to climax. Increasing the intensity and the force would help as well as stimulating other areas of her body, so Conor began kissing her neck while sliding his hands back under her ass to slightly change the way he drove himself into her—and the way she gasped and dug her fingernails into his back told him he was right on. From that point on, all he had to do was keep it up and, less than a minute later, she was quivering and screaming his name, trembling in his arm. Conor held out as long as he could, even though all his cock wanted to do was let it all go.

When her moans died down and she felt weak and limp in his arms, then he ground into her a few more times until his body delivered to him the same gratification Morgan had no doubt felt just moments earlier.

As his body cooled, he slid his hand up her back and held her head to his chest, relishing the feel of her soft hair in his hand. And he didn't care what any of this meant—all he knew was that he would be quite happy if this moment never ended.

Conor's brow was still damp with exertion but a wave of calm flowed over him as Morgan began stirring as if she might be thinking of getting down off the counter. He still marveled, though, at how easily all this seemed to have happened. Once more, not only had he and Morgan gotten past the discomfort from earlier, but they'd also had another amazing bout of sex.

He could get used to this.

"This doesn't change anything," Morgan muttered.

Or not.

In spite of her abrupt dismissal, he laughed. "You're still planning on leaving now?"

"No…but I'm still pissed at you."

"But you'll finish out the day?"

She was silent for a bit before she finally said, "Fine." She pushed against him and slid off the counter to stand on her feet. Then she pulled up her panties and jeans before zipping them and then grabbed her blouse and bra and rushed out of the room.

Conor didn't have nearly that much energy.

He managed to get zipped up again, but that was about it. Leaving the bathroom, he followed her into the bedroom and dropped himself on the bed, the fatigue too great to fight. Her red bra once more covering her breasts, Morgan began rifling through her suitcase on the floor, and Conor couldn't take his eyes off her. Not wanting her to feel self-conscious, though, he peeked through the slits of his mostly closed eyelids to appreciate her. Morgan was so different from Raquel, a woman he used to consider his ideal. Where Raquel was curvy and voluptuous, Morgan was thin and athletic—but she still had curves where they mattered.

Why could he not stop dwelling on thoughts of her—especially when she'd made it clear that he had no chance?

More than that…why did it make him want her all the more?

He had to act like it was no big deal—and there wasn't much time left. He could do anything for a couple of hours…even this.

CHAPTER SIXTEEN

JESUS. WAS CONOR trying to make this as difficult as humanly possible? The only way she'd be able to survive the rest of the day without losing her shit would be to stay focused on *doing* rather than *thinking*.

While she picked up each pair of shoes from the closet to find a space for them in her suitcase, Conor's voice interrupted the quiet.

"There's not much left to the reunion, so you only have to play along for a few more hours."

She continued packing, fighting to keep her voice civil. "What more is there *to* do?"

"I don't know. Some interactive game and prizes. Then lunch and that's it. Oh, yeah. I think Kendra mentioned they'll be taking pictures during lunch, so they're asking everyone to stay till then."

She peeked over her shoulder and saw that Conor seemed to be resting his eyes but actually was fighting to stay awake. Dummy shouldn't have lain down.

She knew how to wake him up.

"So tell me…what happened with you and the washed-up cheerleader anyway?"

"What do you mean?"

"Come on, Conor. I might be *playing* your dumb fucking fiancée who doesn't know what's going on between her man and an old wannabe flame, but don't pretend for a second that I'm actually that stupid." Conor's brown eyes grew wide. Yeah—that woke his ass up.

But he still had the dumb look on his face.

"Seriously, Conor? You're going to act like nothing happened with the bimbo? You *smelled* like her skanky perfume."

"Raquel?"

"Yes, Raquel. She wears the most fucking disgusting shit— some nasty musky floral crap that I can't believe anyone would actually spray on their body. Her sense of smell must have dissipated with her brains." Ah—catty much? It was unbecoming, even of Morgan—and did that mean she was maybe jealous? Packing the last pair of shoes, she added under her breath, "That shit's made out of pig sweat anyway."

"I went to her room for a minute."

Morgan ratcheted it down and started looking in drawers, hoping Conor couldn't read her tone of voice any more than he could see her expression. "What you do is your own business— but I hope to Christ you used a condom with her. I don't want her nasty pussy juice in *my* vajayjay. You know they say you not only sleep with your partners but wi—"

"I didn't sleep with her, Morgan." She turned, seemingly to put clothing in her luggage, but she actually wanted to look at Conor's expression—and it turned out that he looked almost exactly like she'd hoped he would: slightly disgusted but also frustrated. Morgan had long used profanity and other crude language to get under people's skin and push the envelope to see what they were comfortable with. Prissy people didn't stick around to become friends. People with thicker skins got to know Morgan better and wouldn't let her language bother them.

That said, she still could sometimes hit a sore spot—and she could tell by the poorly disguised grimace that she'd gotten to Conor. Whether he thought the imagery was revolting or that she was being unkind to Raquel, Morgan neither knew nor cared. What mattered was that Conor understood her position: she didn't like the idea of being sloppy seconds.

And that green-eyed monster rearing up inside her was going to give away her true feelings if she wasn't careful.

She wasn't even going to dissect the matter inside her head to determine if Conor was actually telling the truth.

"It doesn't matter—and I don't care if you did. I just don't want any of her diseases." She slid the closet door so it closed and then turned around. "Oh, and I'd change my shirt if I were you. You reek of bottled pig sweat." Compulsively, she went to the bathroom one more time to check for items. When she came back in the room, Conor was still sitting on the bed, looking shell-shocked. "What are you waiting for?"

"What do you mean? We have half an hour before the game—no need to rush."

Could this man figure out anything without her? Obviously, she'd made herself too valuable. "Check-out time is eleven, boss. So we're going to need to check out right after the game." She arched an eyebrow to stare him down. "Which means we need to pack *now*, not later."

She could tell all he really wanted was a nap—but no way was she going to let him. This stupid fucking reunion had been his goddamned idea, and he was going to see it through and like it. "Fine." He sat up, grabbing his t-shirt from where he'd tossed it on the bed, and started locating the hole for his head—until he seemed to remember what Morgan had said about the stench on it. He got up and walked over to the dresser, opening a drawer that had his clothes. "I don't know why you call *me* boss when you're the bossy one."

He started laughing until Morgan rewarded him with a pillow slap in the face...and then, after donning the shirt, he started packing.

Good. Wouldn't want to clobber him with the pillow again.

Now that he was focused on packing his suitcase, distracted, Morgan felt like she could breathe. He'd been looking at her with those fucking dreamy eyes of his—and if he couldn't get his head on straight, how would *she* even stand a chance?

Her heart wanted him; her head knew better. And if he could take that same approach, maybe they could make it back to a simple boss-assistant relationship.

"I think I need another coffee. Want one?"

"Nope. All coffeed out."

"Okay. Then I'll be right back."

She didn't really even want a coffee—but she needed time alone to chat with her sister. As she walked down the hall toward the elevator, she pulled up her text messages and typed a short note to her sibling. *Dee, are you free to talk?*

One minute passed, followed by another and another. By the time she reached the bottom of the elevator, she began wondering if she'd have to find someone else to talk with. She had plenty of other friends she could call but not many she wanted to discuss Conor with. After all, Dee didn't know Conor from Adam—but her friends did, and Morgan didn't want her words to taint the way they viewed him or interacted with him...because she wanted to try to find a way to save this friendship.

Finally, as she was walking toward the coffee shop on the first floor of the hotel and scrolling through her contact list, she got a text back from Dee. *Not really. I'm in church with mom. I think they'd frown on me getting up to take a phone call.*

Shit. And church would last way too long. She needed to talk *now* while she had a few moments to herself with the added bonus of the boss being busy. *Okay. Thanks anyway.* As she sent the message, though, she got another one from her sister.

Why? What do you need?

Let's just say it's complicated.

A few seconds passed, and Morgan found the line at the coffee shop by the time her sister sent another text. *Could you be a little more vague?*

Promise not to say anything?

Of course.

The moment of truth. But, first, her coffee order. "Can I get a mocha latte? The smallest you got." The barista nodded and took her money and, before she could throw a tip in the jar, she had another text from her sister. *I'm waiting...*

I slept with Conor.

This had to be the slowest coffee shop ever—but that was okay, because she needed time before she went back to her room. Unfortunately, it was like her sister had disappeared off the face of the earth. Morgan had her mocha latte in hand and decided to find the overstuffed chair around the corner next to a coffee table, because no way was she going back to the room yet.

Say something.

Dee finally texted back. *Sorry. I told you I'm in church. Mom would have noticed I was texting when we're supposed to be praying.* But that was it. Had she read the text where Morgan confessed what she'd done? Would she have to repeat herself? Trying to stop being so damned high strung, she took a sip of her coffee, realizing that wouldn't necessarily help, either, considering she was consuming more caffeine and sugar. Dee finally sent another message. *So why did you sleep with him? Was that part of the deal?*

No!!! Of course not. It just sort of happened.

How could you let something like that happen? Before Morgan could respond, Dee followed up with *Or did you want that?*

Her words gave Morgan pause. *Had* she wanted that to happen? No. No way. Yes, over this extended weekend in tight quarters and weird situations, she'd found herself desirous of her boss, but what about now? When she rationally considered it, was a relationship with Conor what she wanted?

No.

Yes.

Maybe. I don't know. But she had more important things to discuss. *Here's the thing, Dee. Whether I wanted it or not, it happened. Twice. And it's made our relationship feel strained and weird—and I don't know how I feel about working for him anymore.*

But you love that job. You used to always go on and on about how much you loved the work and how awesome Conor was for a boss. You really want to give that up?

Morgan felt better already, just having an opportunity to hash out her emotions with someone who cared about her. *That's what I mean. I really don't know right now. All I know is I'm acting like a stupid jealous girlfriend, but I have no right to do that.*

Um, you slept with him. You have every right. Morgan wanted to tell her more but wasn't sure where to start. Fortunately, Dee asked, *Anything in particular make you feel jealous?*

Yeah. There's this woman here—used to be a cheerleader when they went to school. She didn't give him the time of day until she found out I was his "fiancée" and then she was all over him. And I felt this monster inside me, just ridiculous. Especially when I shouldn't feel that way.

Why shouldn't you feel that way, Mo? You're kidding, right??? You SLEPT with him. Our bodies are wired to get all serious after that. You know this.

Yeah. But I'm not like other women. I shouldn't be feeling this way.

But you do. It's hard to dictate to your brain how your heart should and shouldn't feel, sis.

Morgan took another sip of her mocha latte, savoring the sweet chocolate flavor on her tongue as she let Dee's words sink in. She was right. *Okay, so my feelings have shifted. For some stupid fucking reason, I have deeper feelings for my boss. But I don't know why—especially since we're both acting like it's no big deal.*

So you're saying he doesn't know how you feel.

Right. And no way am I telling him. He's been acting like a dick off and on this weekend.

But you SHOULD!!!

Morgan took another sip. *No, I really shouldn't. He doesn't deserve to know any of that shit, and I don't want him holding it against me.*

Then she waited a minute, followed by another and another...and no response. Yes, she knew Dee was in church and understood that she might not be immediately available, but the waiting was stressing her out, especially since she wondered what Conor might be thinking now that she'd been gone a while. She looked at the time and knew she had to get her ass back up to the room.

Not sure where you went, sis, but text me back when you can. Thanks for talking me down.

Or had she? As Morgan rode in the lonely elevator, she wondered why Dee had given her permission to act like an actual fiancée when she should have virtually slapped the shit out of her.

It wasn't until she got to the door of the room that she got one more text. *Sorry. We're singing now and that might last a while. But I just want to say it again: TELL HIM!*

No fucking way.

She barely had the door closed when Conor asked, "Did they have to milk the cow?"

"What?" Morgan strode across the room to the bedroom doorway.

"Your coffee took a while. Wondered if they had to milk the cow first."

"Oh, funny." But a little honesty wouldn't hurt. "I was texting my sister."

But you'll never know what about.

The area where they'd had all their activities had again been transformed from a dining room with a buffet to a simple room with lots of tables—and the same decorations that had been there since night one. The smell of bacon and coffee lingered, though the steam table and all the dirty dishes had been carted away. When Conor and Morgan walked through the door, good old Kendra handed him two squares of paper—one for him and one for his "fiancée."

"What are these for?"

"Look for the table that has your number on it."

Morgan got close to Conor as they walked all the way inside. "Do we have the same number?"

He handed her one of the pieces of paper. "I don't know. I haven't looked yet."

"Fourteen."

"Me, too." Which made sense. Why would a plus-one want to mingle with people she might not ever meet again and likely had little in common with? The two of them started looking around the room for the table with the lollypop stand in the middle displaying the number they were looking for. When they found it close to the back where Kendra had played announcer that morning, there were already three people sitting there. When Conor saw one face in particular, he did a double take. "Steve Powell? I'd started to think you hadn't made it. Why didn't I see you earlier?"

"Conor? How you been, buddy?" Steve came around the table to where Conor stood and shook his hand. "We just got here today. Our daughter got married yesterday, so we really couldn't miss that."

Ouch. A daughter already getting married and Conor hadn't even committed to a woman yet? When he thought of it that way, it made him feel like a loser. "I guess that explains why I didn't see you at the last reunion, either."

"Yeah. Too many kid issues. But that's why I didn't want to miss today. I won't recognize a soul at our thirty-year reunion."

"You'd think that but it's amazing how many faces I've recognized this time around. It's kind of surreal."

"So what's up with you?"

"Lots. This is my fiancée, Morgan Tredway." Now that the lie was out of the way, he could move on to reality. "Because we're friends on Facebook, you probably already know I own my own accounting business. But what about you, man?"

"I drive trucks. Probably a good thing, because if I was home more, we'd probably have a dozen more kids." Steve had the same short brown hair that went a little past his collar, but Conor had a hard time picturing the guy driving a semi when, back in the day, he'd been all about videogames and computers. He also had the same nasally laugh, and he let it rip until he caught the daggers his wife was throwing him. "Oh, sorry, honey. Do you remember Susan?"

"Susan...*Ruppert?*"

"Not anymore." Conor held out his hand but she came close and gave him a hug. "And this lovely woman is your fiancée? So nice to meet you."

"You, too," Morgan said, and Conor felt his shoulders relax, because it appeared that she already seemed to like Steve's wife better than half his class.

"I guess we all sit around the table?"

As they began choosing seats, Bill Bullock materialized as if by magic, demanding attention, even though the two couples had yet to speak with the other woman already seated there—but her nose was buried in her phone, so there was no hurry.

"Hi, Bill," Conor said, being as polite as possible but irritated that, of all his former classmates at the reunion, he was stuck with this thorn in his side. "And who are you?" he asked the quiet woman at the table.

"Denise Gibson. Conor?" He nodded. "I'm pretty sure we had U.S. History together."

"We sure did. Were you at our ten year?"

"Nope. Kind of like Steve. I had a one-month old newborn and too many expenses to be able to afford coming. But I didn't want to miss it this time."

A squeak of feedback from the microphone at the end of the room showed Brenda Sterling, one of Raquel's old friends, up at the podium. "Hi, everyone. I don't know if you remember me." A couple of guys shouted her name, assuring her that at least *they* recalled her face and now maybe everyone else would remember. "Yeah, that's right: Brenda. I was president of our junior class. But, anyway, are you all ready to play a game?"

There was all manner of clapping, hooting, and hollering— and even Conor joined in—but Morgan, sitting next to him, looked like she'd rather be anywhere else. He wasn't going to let it bother him, but he was paying her, for God's sake. Could she at least *act* like she was having an okay time? He cupped his hand to whisper in her ear. "We're almost done. Chin up, okay?"

She turned her head to look at him and forced a smile, the most sarcastic one Conor had ever seen—and, from Morgan, that was saying something. Stifling a sigh, he hoped his raised eyebrows would communicate that his patience was fading. In response, Morgan made her fake smile even bigger, and Conor shook his head before turning it back to Brenda's voice.

He couldn't help but glance around the room, without turning his head so it would be obvious, to see if Raquel was anywhere to be found. Maybe she'd taken his rejection hard...but, really, what had she expected? For all she knew, Morgan really *was* his fiancée and Raquel had been leading him down the path to perdition via adultery. When they'd kissed, Conor had felt like he was missing something...and he realized Raquel didn't taste like Morgan or feel like her, either—and that was when he'd come running back. Making love with Morgan, he'd thought, sealed the deal. They were a real couple now. But Morgan wasn't having it.

"Oh," Brenda's nasally voice filled the room. "I guess I have to wait a few more minutes because people are trickling in. *Late.* Just like twenty years ago. Report to the principal's office, kids." She snorted at her own joke and a few people around the room gave her some courtesy laughs.

Their table quieted for a few moments as a couple of them looked toward the doors to see who else was coming. Steve finally said, "So no kids, right, Conor?"

"None that I know of." Most of the table laughed at his lame joke like Brenda's a minute earlier. "How many kids do you two have?"

"Four. Our daughter is the oldest and the rest are sons."

Morgan asked, "She got married yesterday, right?" Susan nodded, a proud smile on her face.

Steve turned to Bill. "What about you?"

"Three. All daughters. That would be great except for the child support."

Susan spoke up. "Well, you have to support them one way or another. If you're not sending money somewhere, you're buying them clothes, things for school, food, medicine, school supplies—"

"Yeah, yeah. Did one of my exes put you up to this?"

Conor, hoping to deflect any animosity and ill will Bill might be feeling, turned the spotlight elsewhere. "Denise? What about you?"

"Just my son. He's ten now. Hopefully, weddings and graduations are a little ways off. I'm not ready to stop being a mom."

Bill wiggled his eyebrows. "If you have more kids, your nest stays full."

Frowning, Denise managed to stay civil. "I'd rather focus my money and attention on the little guy I have to make sure he thrives while he's with me and can make it on his own when he leaves. Is that such a bad thing?"

Susan said, "Amen. No matter how many kids you have."

The table was tense, but Steve cut through it like he was wielding a machete. "Hey, Conor, do your parents still have that sign on their bedroom door?"

Conor frowned for a minute, thinking...but after a moment, he recalled seeing it when he and Morgan had gone to his bedroom. Grinning, he replied, "Yeah, they do."

Steve busted out laughing and Susan's face communicated overwhelming curiosity. Before she could say a word, Steve asked, "Morgan, did you die when you first saw that?"

Morgan looked up from the table straight at Steve, and it was clear to Conor that she hadn't seen it when they'd visited on Friday. Sure, he could make excuses but, really, a fiancée probably would have seen that ridiculous embarrassing sign if she'd spent any amount of time with her future in-laws—or they would have talked about it. But it was like she was frozen, unable to speak.

Bill said, "Oh, shit. I remember hearing about that. I gotta give your folks props, man." He held up his hand to high-five Conor while Morgan remained stiff. Slapping Bill's hand, Conor kicked Morgan's foot under the table but no go.

Shit. The ruse was up.

CHAPTER SEVENTEEN

FUCK. MORGAN REALIZED she should know what the guys were talking about—but she'd only been half paying attention, wishing she were anywhere but here...completely done and checked out. "Sorry, what did you say?"

Steve smiled at her. "I just wondered what you thought when you saw the sign on Conor's parents' door. I mean...we guys thought it was funny, but we felt bad for Conor if any girls saw it."

Susan asked, "What was it, honey?"

"You would die."

Morgan started laughing, hoping her acting skills could win her an Oscar that she'd never be able to accept. She gathered it was something that might make some of the women at the table feel uncomfortable. "Yeah...I'm not easily rattled." God, please help her. She had no fucking clue.

"Steve?" Susan prodded.

And he saved the day, as far as Morgan was concerned. "I don't remember exactly. Something like, you know, that old thing: *if the trailer's rockin', don't come knockin'.* Only you could tell the sign was something his dad made."

Conor rolled his eyes but Morgan could see relief in them. He looked over at her, smiling, and said, "If the door's closed, we're busy making Katie and Conor's little brother or sister...so come back later."

But Morgan started laughing hard then, because she *hadn't* seen it. Which was just as bad as being a fucking mannequin—and

144

she had a hell of a hard time imagining Conor's sweet parents hanging a crazy sign like that. *Get it together, girl!* She hoped she could save the day again. "Gets funnier every time I hear it."

"Oh, my God," Susan said. "My hubby's right. I would *definitely* die if my parents had that on their door. Now, maybe not, but back in high school? Oh, my God! Would have shriveled up and died."

Brenda's voice blared through the room again. "Okay, everyone. You'll need to stand up, because under the seat of your chair will be taped a piece of paper with a number on it. Grab it and then tell your tablemates what number you have."

There were two empty chairs at the table but, at this point, Morgan figured those folks had blazed after breakfast. Not that she could blame them, but good riddance. She didn't need to have a bigger audience for the moments when she looked stupid. But why did she care? She'd never see these people again—and, so long as Conor was happy with her performance, she didn't need to give a shit. Conor asked, "What number does everyone have?"

She held hers up and everyone else followed. Everyone had a different number.

Then Brenda said, "Whoever has the number one will be your team leader." Steve pointed to himself with a thumbs up, smiling. "I see a lot of empty chairs, so if no one has a one, then move up to two and three until you have a leader, okay? If you're the team leader, please stand up." Steve obeyed, waiting patiently while other tables slowly had people stand. "Okay, team leaders, please come up here to the front and I'll give you directions."

As if on cue, Raquel plopped down at their table. Morgan felt her hackles rise but relaxed when she saw that even Conor looked a little relieved that the woman was sitting across from them, right next to Bill, instead of closer by. Conor smiled at Raquel, but the woman looked past him as if he were invisible. Damn…that felt cold, even to Morgan, but she wasn't going to say a word. She'd seen Raquel Bettis for who she was the first moment she'd met her. It wasn't Morgan's fault that Conor had allowed himself to be bamboozled like a lovestruck idiot. For a smart guy, he sure could be stupid sometimes.

Then, as if to add insult to injury, Raquel waved—to someone almost directly behind Conor. "Hi, sweetie!"

Morgan couldn't resist turning to see the recipient of Raquel's warm greeting, and she couldn't help feeling like Conor deserved it when she herself joined in the fun by greeting the former quarterback. "Oh, hi, Jacob."

Conor pretended to be distracted by whatever Steve was doing a few feet away, but Morgan knew better. Soon their team leader returned with a small stack of index cards. "Hey. Raquel Bettis, right?"

"Yes. And you are?"

"Steve Powell. I see the blank look in your eyes. Honestly, I could tell you all the stuff I did back in the day, but I wasn't in your circles, so I doubt it would jog your memory." Wow. Morgan had to give the guy credit for being direct. That was ballsy without being butt hurt. She liked it and wondered if Conor would have done that had Raquel not recognized him from the get go. "So you're on our team, right?"

Raquel acted at first like a rabbit caught in headlights, but then she flashed a saccharine smile before holding up her tiny square of paper with the number fourteen on it—but she didn't say a single word.

Steve then asked, "What's your other number, Raquel?"

"*Other* number?"

"It'll be under your chair."

And, as if by some evil master plan, they had a final person join them: Bill's buddy Francis. Ah, now the fun could begin in earnest. Hail, hail, the gang's all here.

Raquel said, "I have a two under my chair."

Francis didn't miss a beat, pulling the paper off the bottom without getting up. "Five."

"Great. So here's how it works, guys. There's a number on the top of each card. I have to ask the person with that number a question. If that's your number, you have to answer it. If you're not a classmate---that is, if you're a spouse," he said, smiling lovingly at his wife before looking at Morgan, "or a fiancée, then you can answer if you know. If not, you'll have to defer to your partner, the person who actually attended school here." There were nods around the table. "So...are we ready?"

Brenda muttered something into the mike and Morgan peeked up front to see a new slide show projected on the wall. The phrase "What's Been Happening?" in a chunky blue font flashed on the screen before new slides of pictures that indicated marriage, babies, cars, and homes.

Steve looked at each person in their group, but their numbers were already on the table, forgotten. "Who's number three?"

Morgan looked around the table before remembering that was her number. "Oh, me!"

"So this will be about Conor since you're his guest." Morgan nodded, resisting the smart-ass urge to tell him she'd figured it out; Conor wasn't the only intelligent person at the table. "How many kids have you—or the classmate, in this case—had since we last saw you?"

"So would this be since the last reunion or since graduation?"

Steve blinked and tilted his head, looking ready to raise his hand or run up to the front to ask for clarification. Morgan was just asking for clarification to be a pain in the ass—so she would also put poor Steve out of his misery. "I can answer both. Now, unless Conor is keeping secrets from me, he's had no children since graduation. But who knows? Maybe he has a secret baby out there that only he knows about. Or maybe he doesn't. *Yet.*" As a finishing touch, Morgan fluffed her fingertips together and deepened her voice while saying, "Mwah-ha-ha-ha-ha-ha-ha."

Steve was taking this game far too seriously now that he was headmaster, but both Susan and Denise began laughing at Morgan's joke that maybe she was being a little evil.

Conor, though, was not amused. Too bad. Even though she planned to keep up with the ruse until they were in the air headed home, no one said she couldn't fuck with him a little. Nothing wrong with making him sweat just a bit.

The torment of the game finally ended so that Conor and all his classmates who were staying at this particular hotel could check out before enjoying a quick lunch. He'd been biting his tongue throughout the game, but Morgan was pushing every one of his buttons. How he'd managed to keep his cool was beyond him— but he was finding it difficult to zip his lips now.

Just get through this. That's what you told Morgan. You're almost done.

Neither said a word as they boarded the elevator, but it had been difficult even getting there, with classmates saying *goodbye* or continuing to reminisce in the hallways. Some of them were leaving before lunch, so there had been hugs and handshakes along the way.

When they got off the elevator on their floor, a wave of relief washed over Conor. They'd almost made it and, even though they had the drive to the airport and then a flight—and, yes, even work tomorrow unless he told Morgan to take a day off—he could see the finish line. Having Morgan play his fiancée had been the stupidest idea ever, and he was tired of paying for it emotionally.

In all fairness, his old buddy Brock had warned him not to "try this at home." Man, had he been right.

Just past the elevator stood Bill and Francis, both looking snide—angry, even. Bill's head was tilted backwards so far that his eyes were slits, his arms crossed in front of his chest. "Why you think you're so high and mighty, Hammond?"

"*What?*"

"Yeah," spat Francis, running a hand through his black hair. "What's your deal?"

"I don't know what you guys are talking about."

"Yeah, you do," said Bill. "You put on this act of being a nerdy guy, right? But here you are with everyone all excited 'cause local boy gets rich, right? And not only do you have your cute little fiancée here—"

"Who's a little too young for you, by the way," Francis interrupted.

"Yeah, a little too young for you."

"And tight."

Conor could feel something foreign inside his gut and his chest, something he imagined hot-headed Morgan experienced on a frequent basis, even if his emotion simmered on a milder scale—but it was anger. No, it was fury. He'd been okay at first—even taken aback, wondering what misdeed he'd committed—but now that these men were accusing him of serious infractions that were, in fact, mole hills, he could feel ire making a home inside him, waiting for him to open the door. "Leave Morgan out of whatever beef you have with me, guys." Ah…his voice sounded calm and cool. Good.

"No, she's involved, whether she wants to be or not." Bill strutted two steps closer to the pair, but Conor wasn't going to back down.

"Morgan, why don't you go to our room and get our things together?"

"No way."

So he would have to deal with her stubborn bossy self, too? Taking a deep breath, he said, "Gentlemen, this thing happens once every decade. I don't know what I could have done in the space of a couple of days to offend you so badly. Let's just let things go and plan to meet again in ten."

"Not that easy, Hammond. You spent the entire weekend cozying up to Raquel, cheating on your fiancée."

"That's bullshit." Dammit. Why couldn't Morgan keep her mouth shut? More than that, why couldn't she even try to act surprised or upset like a real fiancée would?

"My friend Francis here tells me you spent some alone time with Raquel in her room earlier today."

"Now you're spying on me?"

"You're avoiding the question."

Morgan said, "You didn't *ask* a question, dickweed."

Not helping. "You don't know what we were doing in her room and, frankly, it's none of your business."

"I think your fiancée deserves to know."

"Fellas," Morgan jumped back in again, "did you ever think that maybe Conor and I have an open relationship?" She wrapped her arm around his shoulder and winked, her mouth open wide, before giving half a shimmy. "You guys are real fucking brain surgeons."

Even Conor couldn't keep his mouth from gaping. "Morgan, I think I can fight my own battles."

"That true, Hammond?"

"I didn't have sex with Raquel this morning."

"So what happened in there?"

"We...talked."

Francis said, "You hesitated. You're lying."

"Here's the deal, Hammond. You're eating your cake and having it, too." Bill paused, wrinkling his forehead, indicating he knew he'd messed up the saying but not sure how to fix it. "Guys like you—you know, back in the day—you're supposed to end up with a mousy little obedient woman, one who doesn't talk much but keeps a clean house, and you're supposed to be happy with it."

"Where the hell did you get that idea? Is it because you guys are busy paying child support because you couldn't stand being with the women who thought they'd fallen in love with you?"

"You don't fucking come to a reunion to score with the hottest, most wanted chick in our class when you have a girlfriend with a blowjob mouth and succulent tits just ready to blow you."

What? Conor couldn't even believe Bill had been so crass, especially with Morgan right there. "I need you to apologize to my fiancée right now. While I agree that she's beautiful and captivating in every way, you've objectified her like she's a porn star."

"You've treated her worse than I ever could, man."

Put up or shut up time. "I asked you to apologize."

With a sneer, Bill puffed out his chest before crossing his arms. "Make me."

Conor sized him up. He'd never fought anyone physically before, let alone a man bigger than himself—and he wasn't a guy to worry about honor when they were just emotional words being flung around a room to get his goat—but something deep inside himself wanted to prove he could do it. Bill had been an asshole in high school, always engaging in skirmishes or word battles and, even though teachers knew he was an instigator, he'd gotten away with it all four years, usually leaving other kids to pay in one way or another.

No more.

The kid inside Conor wanted justice—and the man Conor had become needed to defend Morgan, even if she didn't care one way or another. He'd asked as politely as possible under the circumstances and Bill had refused. "Fine. I need you to step outside."

Bill raised his eyebrows, an amused look painting his face so much that he seemed to be on the verge of a laughing fit. Francis nodded continuously as if this was something Bill did all the time. "We don't need to go outside, man, 'cause this won't last long. Take your best shot and then I'll lay you out."

How the hell had he gotten himself into *this* predicament? And was there a diplomatic way out?

CHAPTER EIGHTEEN

LIKE IT OR not, Conor had been pulled into a fight and he wondered how the hell some men did this all the time, especially once they'd matured. Conor dug deep in his memory, back to a time when his dad had tried to teach him how to defend himself, trying techniques he knew he'd never use. But dad, being the smart man he'd always been, knew the lessons would come in handy someday. He clenched both hands at his side as if warming up, and then he consciously formed the fist his dad had taught him to make—solid and strong. Moving one more step toward Bill, he kept his legs apart to balance his center of gravity. *Punch with your whole body, not just your hand.*

Taking a deep breath, Conor pulled his fist back and let it fly before it landed squarely on Bill's jaw.

Holy shit. He'd done it.

Bill blinked a few times, as if he hadn't expected it. Conor kept his face neutral but *shit*. His knuckles hurt like hell. But he also remembered dad's advice to defend himself, too, so he brought both fists up in a fighting stance again, ready to deflect Bill's swing that was surely coming.

There were two quick punches—and the second one connected with his jaw despite his defensive posture, knocking him on his ass. And if he'd thought his hand hurt, his jaw let him know that that was nothing. He knew he had to get up, though. He hadn't passed out and he wasn't bleeding profusely. No teeth had been knocked out; no bones were broken. He needed to get up and fight some more. That's what guys did, right?

As Conor was lifting himself up off the floor, Francis said, "Bill, there's Kendra and some dude in a suit heading our way. We better get out of here before they get here. Remember that bill we had to pay in Vegas?"

Bill snarled, assessing the now-upright Conor. After a brief face-saving pause, he said, "Guess today's your lucky day, Hammond. But think about what I said."

Morgan was holding onto his arm. "Are you okay?"

As the men darted into the stairwell doorway, Conor asked, "What did Bill say that he wants me to think about? I can't remember."

"Something moronic, no doubt."

Kendra and the man in the suit that Francis had warned Bill about before they skedaddled showed up next to them. The woman was not her usual bubbly self, however, and Conor suspected it was because they were ruining her perfect event. "Conor, do you want to tell me exactly what happened?"

"Not particularly."

Morgan, however, had no qualms about talking. "Bill Bullock was being an absolute pig, commenting crudely about my body, using offensive language, and Conor defended my honor. For that, Bill punched him in the face, knocking him down."

"Are you okay?"

Conor was rubbing his jaw with his left hand, not that it helped any. He'd nurse the knuckles later. "I've been better."

"Can we get you anything?"

"No. We just need to check out now."

"You're planning to stay for lunch, right?"

Morgan stepped in again. "That had been the plan, but it's all up to Conor. We'll see how he's feeling after checking out."

"Yeah, we'll be staying."

Kendra and the man left and then Morgan and Conor walked the rest of the way to their room. The caring, albeit bossy, way Morgan had been acting, he figured they were on better terms, especially now that she knew he wouldn't put up with that shit from a man acting *like a pig*, as she'd put it.

But he was wrong.

As soon as the door shut behind them, Morgan asked, "What the fuck were you thinking, Conor? Newsflash: You're not in sixth grade. No more playground fights with the class bully."

"Yeah, and what would you have said if I'd just let him trash talk you?"

"I can defend myself, you know."

"Maybe you don't realize it, but Bill was challenging my masculinity—even if he *was* insulting *you*. You'll have to take my word for it here, okay?" Morgan rolled her eyes and started opening drawers in the chest of drawers across from the sofa. "We already checked everything. We're good to go."

"Yeah, and that's how I lost my favorite pair of earrings a long time ago. It doesn't hurt to check one last time." Conor nodded, trying to be sympathetic, but it wasn't happening. As the pain subsided ever so slightly, he allowed a foreign emotion to wash over him.

He'd been a tough guy this morning—just once in his life, he'd been a bit of a brute, defending his woman's honor in hand-to-hand combat. He hadn't won the fight, but he also hadn't lost, and so a primal reaction took hold of his brain.

He'd done what any man would have.

"You're not even gonna ask me how?"

Jolted out of his moment of silent self-praise, Conor asked, "What?"

"How I lost my earrings."

"Sure. How?"

"I was a kid, and my parents took us on a weekend vacation to the beach. I'd never been in a hotel before, so it was exciting to unpack my entire suitcase to fill the closet and drawers, just like this was *my* bedroom for the weekend. The morning we had to go, dad kept telling me to pack and, of course, I told him I was working on it. But I forgot to check the drawer by the bed where I'd tossed my earrings, and it wasn't until we were at our next destination—camping in the mountains with my aunt, uncle, and their kids—that I remembered. Dad said we weren't going back, and we weren't heading that way when all was said and done. He said it would teach me a valuable lesson.

"And it did. I triple-check hotel rooms before I check out now."

"*Triple-check?* Isn't that excessive?"

"Maybe…but I haven't lost anything since."

"Then have at it."

Morgan growled, "Like I need your permission."

Shit. She was still grouchy. Maybe having some lunch, knowing they'd be heading out soon, would help her chill out. If food were the way to a man's stomach, perhaps it would be the way to a woman's zen. There was only one way to find out.

Conor had attended a business conference here and there but determined years ago that they were a huge waste of money and time. Even the networking opportunities didn't make them profitable ventures. In fact, the only thing that made them worthwhile was that they were business write offs out of town.

But one thing he didn't understand was why hotels didn't change check-out times to coordinate with the events they hosted. He understood that people still had to get out so the rooms could be cleaned for the next batch of guests but it was damned inconvenient.

There was no sense in complaining, though. They'd be feeding them one final time—and this would be his last chance to say goodbye to a good many folks he wouldn't see for another ten years, if he even bothered coming to the next one.

"Hey, guys!" The voice behind them sounded friendly and familiar, but he wasn't sure who it was until he turned around.

"Hi, Amber. Leaving now or are you sticking around for the rest of the reunion?"

The woman laughed like Conor had just told the funniest joke, throwing her head forward so that her blonde ponytail whipped over her head. Then she straightened her spine and said, "I still *live* here, remember?"

"Yeah, I forgot." Morgan gave Amber a polite smile but kept her mouth shut. "Sorry. I know not everyone moved away."

"That's cool. But, yes, I'm sticking around till the end."

"So…if you stayed in a room," Morgan said, "why are you checking out?"

"My parents. They're watching my youngest and wanted me to have a 'vacation,' so they paid for two nights in the hotel. Anyway, I thought some of talking to the gals running the show to see if they want some help next time." They took a step closer to the counter. One more person left to check out and then it was their turn. "Not that they did a bad job. It was great! But I thought they might like more help, and it looked like fun." She lowered her voice and got close to Conor—and Morgan didn't even bat an eyelash—as if she were revealing a state secret. "And maybe I could get a discount on the cost of this shindig. Know what I mean?"

Conor smiled. "I'm sure they wouldn't object to more help. When I see what all they arranged here, I can't imagine the time and effort it took to put it together."

"For reals." After a second, she added, "I don't know if Kendra really likes me, though."

"What does that have to do with it?"

"Would *you* want to work with someone you didn't like?"

He'd only had to do that in a work-study job in college, but it wasn't a big deal. You went in, got your job done, minded your own business. "Don't you think we're past all the petty high school baloney?"

"Maybe, but I'm talking about the way she treats me now. I don't know. Maybe you're right."

If it were Conor, he'd take all the volunteer labor he could get—and, having seen the way Kendra had run around like a chicken with her head cut off, smiles and all, he doubted she'd turn down help. "All you can do is ask."

Amber nodded and got a little too close for comfort, but Morgan was doing a shitty job of playing jealous fiancée now. At this point, she was just phoning in her performance, biding her time till they left—and Conor didn't know if pulling her aside and talking with her would help—in fact, he felt certain it would make things worse.

Amber wasn't trying to horn in that way anyway—at least, Conor didn't think so. Giggling, she poked him with her elbow and said, "Might want to keep an eye on your wife-to-be, though. Sounds like she's keeping her old flames close."

Conor wasn't quite sure what she meant by that, but he could tell the other woman was fishing for something. She probably doubted the whole ruse, because both Conor and Morgan had turned out to be shitty actors. They were almost through the reunion, so he knew they could make it to the end, but the last thing he wanted was for Amber to continue poking at him. Meanwhile, Morgan looked up from her phone with a bored expression. "Remember? I told you I made it sound like I'd been dating my ex recently and confused the heck out of Amber?" Morgan's eyes had flared with anger until Amber turned, and then Morgan's demeanor appeared to be as sweet as could be.

And, yes, he remembered her first night's screw up.

There was one way to distract Amber—and maybe the same technique would shut Morgan up and keep that nasty look off her face.

Besides, Conor couldn't resist.

He slid his hand against her cheek until the hair above her ear wrapped around his fingers. The shock in her eyes mingled with a flash of anger, but she didn't fight him as he pressed his mouth against her warm lips. Her eyes might have shown irritation, but her mouth communicated passion and fire—and little resistance.

Would they ever be able to return to their normal friendship, their boss-employee relationship?

Morgan might find a way to, but Conor would never be able to forget the way her body felt up against his, the way she smelled up close, the way her mouth tasted.

"Can I help you, ma'am?"

As Amber turned to face the registration desk, Morgan pulled herself from his kiss. She gave him a little glare before burying her head in her cell once more. With Amber preoccupied with the front desk, Conor began thinking about Morgan and her ex. She'd called him something sickening like *Sexy Rexy*, but it hadn't bothered Conor in the past.

Now, though…the thought of Morgan spending any time with another man, but especially with that sleazeball, made him want to beat the shit out of the guy.

What the hell was wrong with him? He'd thrown a punch and taken two and now all of a sudden he was resolving to end all his conflicts that way?

Well, it came down to one very important fact: Rex didn't deserve someone like Morgan.

Then again, neither did Conor. And it was probably too damn late to try to convince her otherwise.

*　　*　　*

As Morgan created a deluxe ham-and-cheese sandwich with veggies and mustard, she could feel Conor just behind her doing the same thing. What was going through his mind she couldn't even pretend to know—but she knew what *she* was thinking. This lunch was her last obligation before she could go back to just being Conor's assistant.

But she wasn't sure she wanted to anymore.

Maybe it was true that you couldn't go home again, and it felt doubly true as far as returning to their old life. She doubted things between them would ever be the same.

Conor had shown her a side of himself that she'd never seen. Yes, she'd known for years that he was a bit of a player and he'd told her he'd been a nerd in school. Those things weren't surprising or even upsetting, and they made Conor the man he'd become. It was the other qualities, the ones she hadn't expected, that had her thinking twice about *everything*. Over the course of the weekend, Conor had been arrogant, brash, and a bit of an asshole, and she wasn't liking it. And even knowing she had a bit of a double standard in that she might have kind of liked one of her boyfriends being a bit medieval by fighting to save her honor, she hadn't expected that behavior from Conor. He'd been the one man she'd always known who kept his basest self in check—and yet, this morning, he'd proved her wrong, because he'd let it all out.

The animal out of the cage, so to speak...and it wasn't pretty.

And she was pretty sure none of these behaviors had been an act. This was the *real* Conor, one she'd never seen because she'd only spent forty hours a week around the guy before. Once his professional persona dropped, this was the real him—and she didn't much care for the real man.

As she used the tongs to toss several potato chips on her plate, she wondered if she had it all wrong. Maybe this extended weekend had changed him, and she analyzed that idea as she looked over the giant cookies, trying to decide if she'd take one or skip it. The confrontation with Bill, for example. Conor might not have gotten in fistfights with people over the years since she'd begun working for him, but he *had* always been a little arrogant, often shown a prick-y side that made him look like an utter jerk. Maybe it had been easier for her to dismiss before because she could go home every night. The more she thought about it, she thought maybe the weekend's behavior was just Conor's personality on steroids—and, if she was correct, Morgan believed there would be no turning back. Now that Conor had gotten a taste of his power, he'd never go back to the mellower version of his self.

Which meant she wouldn't be able to stand him.

She slid over to the drink station and poured a glass of iced tea, aware the whole time that Conor was right behind her. "Where do you want to sit?"

"I don't care. Wherever. It's *your* reunion." She turned and scoped out the room, immediately regretting her statement. She saw three people she wanted nothing to do with—Raquel, Bill, and Francis, though both men were heading to a corner of the room, trying not to be obvious while making sure they got their money's worth. Technically, Morgan was still on the clock, so she'd tolerate whatever place Conor chose to sit.

Conor's eyes seemed to linger on Raquel, and it took everything Morgan had not to say a word. But he let the air out of his lungs and kept looking around, his expression perking up when he saw Steve waving at them to come over. Morgan plastered that same fakey smile on her face as she followed Conor over to their table but, by the time they sat down, the Mona Lisa curve of her lips was as genuine as could be.

Because she had made a decision. As soon as they got back home, Morgan was giving her two weeks' notice.

CHAPTER NINETEEN

GETTING OUT TO the parking lot proved to be quite an effort, while Conor hugged more people and shook more hands than he had during his entire high school career. And he wasn't going to say it aloud, but he was keeping an eye out for Raquel. At this point in the proceedings, he knew he didn't want a woman like her as a partner or even a girlfriend, but the baser part of him deep down inside wanted one last chance to make that determination, to decide if he was one-hundred percent certain. Right now, for some stupid reason, his interactions with her felt unfinished.

There was no Raquel, but he did get to say goodbye to the likes of Amber and Kyra and Denise and Kendra and dozens of other classmates.

And then Steve and Susan.

"Man, we can't go twenty years without seeing each other again."

Conor agreed. "You're right."

"I don't want to insert myself into your lives," Susan said, touching Morgan's shoulder (and Morgan didn't object), "but we'd love to attend your wedding. Now that the kids are older, we can get away with traveling on occasion without them." Morgan's face was like granite, even though she made a smile pop up on her face, but surely Susan could read that something was amiss. "Oh, but if you're doing something small…"

Conor said, "We'd love to have you guys there. Hell, Steve, I should have you be a groomsman."

Steve's face told Conor all he needed to know—that time and distance had not weakened their friendship at all. "I would be honored." Morgan nodded, but her acting skills sucked.

She wasn't even trying anymore.

Susan said, "If you guys are ever in our neck of the woods, we'd be happy to have you—anytime."

Morgan finally seemed to get with the program. "Where do you guys live?"

"Florida. Just outside Miami. And I agree with Susan—we'd love to have you anytime."

"Same to you both. If you're ever in Washington, give us a ring."

As the two couples began making their way through the lobby, Bill and Francis came near again—and Conor felt his hackles rise. He really didn't want to get into it again with those guys. Patting Steve on the back, he said, "Safe travels. Are you flying out?"

"Out of Vegas. We're driving to Nevada, spending an entire week playing tourist. We're going to hang in Utah a bit and then we're checking out the Hoover Dam before hanging in Vegas for a couple of days."

"Sounds fun." The two men shook hands and Susan hugged Morgan, leaving them open to the approach of the terrible twins. Conor readied himself in case he had to bloody his knuckles again, but both men appeared to be calm. When they got closer, though, Bill didn't approach *him*; instead, he faced Morgan. "Hey...I wanted to apologize to you." Unlike his usual brash self, Bill was calm, his voice quiet. "Conor was right. I crossed a line."

"I accept your apology. Thank you."

Then Bill turned to face Conor. "You, though, man...I oughta knock one of your teeth out, just for good measure." Conor felt his hackles rise and prepared once more to duke it out, much as he didn't want to. But then Bill added, "Just messin' with ya. I had a little too much to drink over this whole shindig, including this morning. I guess I just let it get the best of me." He stuck out his hand. "No hard feelings?"

Well...if Morgan could accept their apology after the shitty things they'd said about her, Conor certainly could. "Yeah, okay."

Just as he brought his hand closer to Bill's to shake it, the other man withdrew his. "Gotcha."

Still an asshole.

"Yep. See ya in ten years."

Not if Conor could help it.

Climbing into the rental car a few minutes later, Conor tried not to act disappointed. He'd been able to say goodbye to so many people, but he hadn't seen Raquel again. As he'd told himself earlier, it wasn't like he wanted a woman like that as a mate or even a girlfriend, but his baser self wanted one last chance to make that determination.

Well, there was always Facebook.

And then it dawned on him…he hadn't even *looked* for her at lunch. Maybe she *had* been there.

What did that mean? Was it because of Morgan? Had he been too worried about whatever weird thing was happening between him and his assistant that Raquel had been the furthest thing from his mind?

"What time is our flight?" Morgan asked.

She already knew the answer. "Not till this evening."

"Oh, joy. More time alone with nothing to do."

God, she was being a bitch, but maybe he deserved it. He wasn't so sure anymore. "I want to see my parents one more time before we go. I won't get to see them again until Thanksgiving."

"Fine."

The atmosphere in the SUV was thick, like pea soup that has cooled, and as heavy as a lead jacket. Part of Conor wanted to talk, to find out what was eating at Morgan, because he'd thought her mood would improve once they left the reunion and she no longer had to portray his fiancée—but, if anything, her demeanor had soured.

And, even though the other part of Conor wanted nothing to do with it, the rational side of him prevailed and decided to talk. "What's wrong, Morgan?" he asked at the stoplight.

He couldn't see her face because she was looking out the passenger window. "Nothing."

Bullshit. Staring at the red light in front of them, he assessed her attitude. Men might not be outwardly emotional or instinctive creatures, but there was no denying the cold breeze flowing off her. Conor felt like he needed a coat inside the car. "You want to talk?"

"Not really."

Even though he'd never seen Morgan this closed off, he knew

better than to pursue it when she'd communicated that she wanted to be left alone, and he understood that anything he said right now would be like gasoline on a fire, one he wasn't in the mood to try to put it out.

So let it burn.

"Morgan, I wanted to thank you for helping my Conor stay organized. I know he's tried his whole life to be able to do that himself, but he'd always get sidetracked by more interesting things." Conor's mom held up the pitcher of iced tea, her eyebrows raised in silent question.

Morgan nodded, letting her know a little more would be fine. The caffeine would help her stay awake until they boarded the plane. "He's still the same way. In all fairness, though, it's hard to make a huge mess in his business. But all the files are on his computer, so even when he's not organized there, we can search and find."

Conor said, "I'm not as bad as both of you think, although I have reformed. Morgan set up a solid filing system on our network, so it's just a matter of me putting things where she expects to find them."

"Yes, but let's just say you get a little creative with your files."

"You don't seem to have any problems finding them."

"Only because I've gotten to know you so well." Wow. That was true. Morgan felt like she knew Conor almost as well as she knew her friends. Definitely better than she knew half the guys she'd dated since working for him. That was probably why she'd been so damned disappointed at his behavior over the past few days, leading her to believe that he'd reverted to his *real* self—and the guy at work was simply an image. "Mrs. Hammond?"

"Please call me Dale."

"Okay, Dale," Morgan nodded, her finger tracing a pattern in the condensation on the glass. "Conor's old classmates said you have a crazy sign on your bedroom door, one they all seemed to remember fondly."

His mother began laughing. "The old *if this trailer's rocking* sign?"

"Well, yeah, but they hinted that it was a little more suggestive than that." She tried to recall the exact words they'd used.

"I know. His father made that stupid thing years ago, but I took it down a while back."

"Why, mom? I thought you guys loved it."

"No, your *dad* did. Thought it was funny. And I did, too, but it served its purpose."

Morgan brought her glass to her lips, hoping not to give away her thoughts by her expression. Did his mom mean they were no longer interested in sex? Would she herself eventually lose interest due to old age?

"What purpose, mom? To embarrass the crap out of us kids?"

His father shouted from the living room, "That was just a fringe benefit."

"Thanks, dad."

Mrs. Hammond said, "Your dad had all kinds of things in our room, like his gun collection. Even though the guns were locked up, he didn't want kids getting any bright ideas, like stealing his things to get easy money. He figured if you all pictured us having sex in there, you'd stay out. After all, if a parent would hang a sign like that on the door, heaven knew what they'd actually *do* in the room."

The giggles started pouring out of Morgan's mouth slowly at first, but as the joke washed over her, the laughter gained momentum. Soon, his mom and Conor joined in and even his dad started laughing in the other room.

Wiping tears from her cheeks, Morgan said, "Seems like an awful lot of trouble to go to just to deter teens from looking through your stuff."

"Maybe...but it worked."

Morgan began laughing again, even harder when she noticed that Conor wasn't as amused as she.

His father got up and was walking through the dining room toward the kitchen, but he paused. "Son, tell me what happened to your jaw again. You got in a fight?"

"Yeah. That happens sometimes, right?"

"You never did this kind of thing in high school and now, in your thirties, you're throwing punches. Don't you think it's a little late in the game to start doing that?"

"It didn't last long because I followed the advice you gave me back then—you know, about how to fight."

"*Back then.* Son, maybe you shouldn't be going to these reunions if it brings out the kid in you."

Conor's jaw slackened and Morgan had to stifle a belly laugh. Her boss seemed mute.

"Ed, knock it off. You know he wouldn't have done it unless absolutely necessary. Conor's not a fighter."

"These guys were always bullies—but it came down to him or me. He was insulting Morgan. I'm not even going to repeat the nasty things he said. I was defending her honor."

As much as Morgan didn't want to back him up today, she felt compelled to set the record straight. "It's true. The guy was being crass and disgusting—and I can usually take that kind of thing, but Conor asked him to apologize and he refused and told him to take his best shot. So he did."

"You would have done the same for me, Ed."

Conor's father shook his head, as if giving up the argument. "Well, at least it looks like you won the fight."

"I don't know about that. But they left. That's all that matters."

"Mama can bandage your wounds if you want, honey."

Morgan could tell from Conor's response—not what he said but the way he said it—that he was probably ready to head back home. "That's okay, mom. I think I'll live."

He might have been tired of his parents already, but Morgan had enjoyed meeting them—and she knew she was going to miss them…probably a thousand times more than she'd miss Conor after she quit. They would have made great in-laws for real.

Soon, though, they were at the airport. As usual, it bustled with people and activity, but here they were, stuck in a TSA line. Morgan hadn't been able to help smiling and hugging Conor's parents when they'd said goodbye, because they were sweet people who had no idea what an ass their son had become. In fact, Morgan had started to grow quite fond of them, but it had taken every ounce of decorum she had to manage to treat Conor civilly while they'd been there.

He just didn't fucking get it.

Clueless.

So everywhere they went, she kept her head stuck in her phone, and that managed to help her keep her mouth shut. From the car rental place to the airport shuttle, she'd barely looked at Conor twice. And she thought maybe he'd taken the hint, because he'd barely been talking.

She was in no mood to chat.

Finally, they'd made it through all the preliminary stuff and just had to wait to board the plane, but they had two hours to go before their flight. "Why don't we grab a bite, Mo?"

Mo. Hmph. Trying to be all buddy-buddy now?

"Whatever you want."

No one said she had to look up from her phone.

She continued to follow him, her phone in her left hand while pulling her overstuffed bag on the right, her purse draped over her shoulder. As they walked down the tiled space, she smelled roasted coffee beans followed by the smell of baked bread and then a sweet chocolate scent. That was soon replaced by the aroma of barbecue and pizza.

All that deliciousness, and Conor led her to a sandwich shop. Probably just as well, though, because she didn't know that she wanted something heavy in her belly before the flight. But when he ordered, he asked first for two glasses of beer. "To start." Then he asked, "What do you want to eat?"

"Whatever."

"Hmm."

"I'll find us a place to sit." Maybe then he'd get the hint. She found a small table tightly packed in with a dozen others and realized there was no escape from the general noise of the airport. That was okay, because it wasn't like she felt like talking anyway. Conor rolled his bag to the table and then went back to the counter. When he returned with a tray full of chips and sandwiches, Morgan made sure her face was still buried in her phone, communicating in no uncertain terms that she wanted nothing to do with conversation.

But when she got an unexpected text, she spoke when she excused herself to go to the ladies' room.

Conor was already sick of Morgan's shitty attitude, but he realized they needed some time away from each other. They'd never spent this much time together in such a short span, and he figured Morgan would do better away. He planned to give her Monday off to recover, hoping she'd be fresh and happy come Tuesday.

What a strange weekend it had been.

Maybe she was mad that he hadn't made any commitments to her, even though they'd slept together twice. But Morgan had flat-out told him not to even go there.

Then again, women could be fickle. He knew this.

Taking a long pull on his beer, he looked out of the small, tight restaurant. People wandered past, not whizzing by like frenzied crowds as they would closer to the gates. Here, they hung out, digging in for the long wait before their flight.

He could relate.

As he lifted his glass again, his eyes locked with one passenger sauntering past.

Raquel.

And her blue eyes met his at the same time his landed on hers. Her face immediately brightened and she and her rolling bag sashayed into the little restaurant.

At this point, Conor had nothing to lose. If he and Morgan had been on speaking terms, he would have politely wished Raquel a nice flight and said he looked forward to seeing her again in ten years. But Morgan had made it more than clear that there was nothing between them, so Conor had no shackles holding him back.

He stood, meeting her in a warm embrace. No, she wasn't Morgan, but the musky floral perfume wafting from her pulse points helped Conor realize she was a port in the storm nonetheless.

"Imagine meeting you here, sweet Conor Hammond."

"I could say the same thing."

"Where's your fiancée?"

"She had to use the facilities." Raquel nodded, a cool expression frozen on her face. "You can join us here until your flight."

"Oh, no. I'm not about to piss off Maureen. But—" she said, touching Conor's forearm, "I get the feeling not all's happy in paradise, so I wanted to make a bit of a proposition." Conor didn't know what to say, so he simply raised his eyebrows and opened his ears. "Not all married men are faithful, Conor. I know my husband wasn't. So I just wanted to let you know that I have lots of time and plenty of frequent flyer miles, okay? And I'd love to see you anytime you feel like it."

Conor didn't even know what to say, but he imagined Morgan showing up right now, pissed off in general, ready to engage Raquel like he had Bill hours earlier.

As Raquel fished through her purse, she asked, "So what happened to your face?" His knuckles and jaw had stopped throbbing and the swelling had gone down, although there was a general soreness in those areas. He wondered if Raquel found that sexy, unlike Morgan.

"Bill Bullock."

"What happened?"

"He was being a dick, acting like he did twenty years ago, and we got in a bit of a fight."

"*Ooh*. I'm sorry I missed that." Her lips curled in a smirk, but she looked down, writing on a piece of paper in a tiny notepad. A few seconds later, she ripped the paper off and, after tucking the notepad and pen back in her purse, she slid her fingers into Conor's palm, pressing the folded paper into his hand. "Here's my number if you ever want to talk…or anything else."

As he watched Raquel's fine ass sway away from him, he wondered if he'd died and gone to heaven. The ultimate woman—the ideal when he'd been in school—had just propositioned him. Could life ever get any better than this?

CHAPTER TWENTY

IN THE PRIVACY of a quiet bathroom stall, Morgan allowed herself to read the text from Rex, her asshole ex...the one who broke up with her because she wore too much red.

Dick.

But she couldn't believe what she was reading now. *Hey, Morgan. I wanted you to know this time apart has made me realize how much you mean to me. I miss you. And I want to be your T-Rex again. You were the light of my life, and I don't care if you wear red 7 days a week. I just need you in my life. I promise to make it all up to you.*

Morgan read and reread his text, confusion washing over her like a steady rain. Last week, would she have given Rex a second chance, maybe one he didn't deserve?

But, more than that, did she even love him anymore? Had she ever loved him?

And what about Sandra, his new girlfriend?

As much as her emotional side wanted to react immediately, she knew she needed to let her emotions cool so she could think about it rationally. She'd been in touch with her heart all day long, and it had to stop. That was the main reason why she hadn't been talking—because she couldn't trust herself to not say something she'd regret later. Even if she quit tomorrow, she'd still need Conor to be a reference—and being a bitch wouldn't work in her favor.

She just couldn't trust herself.

So, when she exited the bathroom and began walking back to

the restaurant, she nearly leapt out of her skin when she saw Raquel. Seeing that greedy man-eating bitch made Morgan immediately forget her higher purpose.

But, as she marched toward the restaurant, Raquel shook hands with Conor and left, walking in the opposite direction—and Morgan didn't know if she felt relieved or frustrated.

Even Conor looked confused as she approached their table.

"What was *that* all about?" she asked, picking up her beer and polishing it off.

"I'm not sure." Maybe that was true, but he opened a piece of paper he'd been holding in his hand and stared at it for a long time.

Setting Rex aside, though, Morgan knew what she had to do. "Conor, I need to get something off my chest now."

"What's that?"

Well, her news would have the added benefit of wiping the stupid look off his face. "I'll train my replacement...but I'm giving you a four-week notice that begins now."

"*What?*"

"Do you need that in writing?"

She couldn't read his expression. "No, I just want to know why. Is it because of Jacob?"

"What? *No!*" She got up from the table, storming to the bar to order another beer. Getting away from Conor for a few minutes would help her keep her emotions on a steady, even keel, because they'd already started escalating. Why the fuck couldn't she just be cold and rational?

When she returned, Conor was no longer sitting at the table. "Why are you leaving, Morgan? After all these years, I think I deserve an explanation at the very least. If it's because of someone you met here—"

"Shut the fuck up, Conor," she hissed. God, he was clueless. How the hell had she fallen in love with her boss, a man who might have been a gaming nerd in his high school days but who now hid behind a wealthy playboy façade? She'd fallen for the guy underneath it all, the man his parents and friends adored. But maybe the man he appeared to be now wasn't a façade at all. Maybe it was completely real, and this weekend had put him out on full display. So, whether or not she hated what a jerk Conor had become, she hated herself even more for allowing herself to fall in love with him.

Dumb girl.

But there was no way she'd let Conor know what she was thinking inside—and vitriol would easily throw him off the scent. "That's how fucking stupid you are." She felt her eyes begin to well up with tears. Where the hell had they come from? "You just don't get it." Fighting the weepy feeling consuming her, she downed half the new beer in a few gulps as she tried to figure out exactly why she needed to leave Conor's employ. It wasn't Rex...but now she felt confused, an emotion she hadn't felt in a very long time.

Morgan's unexpected news winded Conor more than the punch Bill had delivered earlier that day, and as the swelling and pain was disappearing from those wounds, his pretend fiancée was attempting to deliver her own blows in a much more sinister way.

If she needed to grow—or maybe if she got an offer she couldn't refuse from one of his classmates—he'd understand, but he couldn't counter another job proposal if she wouldn't be straight up with him. What the hell had he missed today?

Suddenly, Morgan picked up her cell phone and started tapping on the screen. "How can you text at a time like this?"

"Can you give me five minutes, please?"

What the hell? It was like the airport was another country. So he picked up the folded piece of paper from Raquel. On it, she'd written her name and phone number, and then she'd added something at the bottom, something Conor didn't know how he would have reacted if she'd given it to him, say, Friday night. *My lips, your manhood. All you have to do is call.* XOXO She'd also drawn a heart.

The flattery puffed up his ego, but he knew it wasn't real. Raquel was looking for a sugar daddy and, because of Conor's temporary stupidity (Morgan was right, after all), he'd fallen for it. Raquel only cared about one person—herself. Would he love her lips around his manhood? Hell, yeah. What man wouldn't? And she would gladly spend his money. But would she love him? No. And a year ago, he wouldn't have given a shit.

Two weeks ago, he wouldn't have given a shit, either.

That left him with grappling with these strange new feelings for Morgan. He'd realized over this weekend that he cared for her a lot more—and much more deeply—than he ever would have thought possible. Losing her would be like taking one of his limbs—and not just because she was a hell of an assistant.

Dare he say it?

There were sparks there that he wanted to fan, wanted to coax into a blazing inferno—but he knew Morgan wasn't interested. And, if she left his business, he'd have no chance at all.

Morgan slapped her phone on the table and slid it over to him. "There."

"What?"

"Just read it."

Conor's eyes focused on the flat surface of her smartphone and saw that her texting app was open. Oh—Rex. The dirtbag. Conor had never understood that relationship to begin with, but what did he know? "You're the *light of his life?*"

"Keep going."

Morgan's final response was terse compared to Rex's long flowery text. *I don't love you, Rex. There's someone else, so don't text me anymore.*

That was a blow that hurt worse than the one to his jaw. The physical pain was already subsiding. How long would it take for this internal one to ease up? "I *knew* it. Please don't tell me it's Bill or Francis. Anyone but those guys."

Morgan looked like she would have shot him if she'd had a gun in her hand. "Really, Conor? Are you that fucking dumb?"

There was one other possibility in his heart, but he dared not hope.

No, he needed to. If he'd learned anything over this weekend, it was to take chances, even when the outcome wasn't guaranteed. And what did he have to lose?

Nothing…because Morgan had already given her notice.

On a whim, Conor got off his stool and on one knee. Morgan's facial expression changed from sour and pissed off to almost amused. "Morgan Tredway, I had no idea until this ridiculous weekend that I love you. I've always loved you, but I thought it was from a sense of gratitude because you've been a godsend to me and the business. But that's not it. I love your sense of humor, your attitude, your outspokenness. If you need to leave, then leave." Morgan opened her mouth, ready to reply, but

Conor wasn't finished, and he took one of her hands in his. "But if you stay, I want you to be my real fiancée."

Morgan blinked then, appearing to be at a loss for words.

"If you were the light of Rex's life, then you're the disco ball of mine." Morgan's eyebrows jumped up her forehead and her eyes lit up—but he couldn't tell if she was amused or angry. "I know I haven't been myself this weekend."

"Got that right. You've been a huge ass."

"Fair enough. Can I make it up to you?"

Morgan's beautiful green eyes searched his, making Conor see the future in his mind. A life spent with this woman would be a life worth living to the fullest—and it felt right. She was already his right-hand woman in every way imaginable and, thanks to the shenanigans they'd engaged in over the weekend, he'd discovered that no one else could play her role as the woman by his side.

But, of course, the final decision was up to her.

A small smile curled on her lips, lighting up her eyes before rounding her cheeks. "I think that would be the best ending to this insane weekend."

Conor stood then, her hand still in his, and she joined him. "Does your pretend engagement ring work or do you want a different one?"

"Are you kidding? This rock is gorgeous."

Conor cupped his hands on the sides of her face and pulled her into a slow kiss, savoring her sweetness, hardly able to believe that this woman had just agreed to be his wife. Then he said, "I guess, as my assistant, I can have you work on planning the wedding."

"We have to set a date first. And, besides, you forgot I gave you my notice."

"You still want to leave the business?"

Morgan scrunched up her lips in thought before replying. "That depends."

"On what?"

"Do I have to go into the office tomorrow?"

Conor laughed. "I think we both need Monday off—because we have a lot of making up to do."

Morgan giggled and kissed him on the cheek. Then she said, "We need to get to the boarding area if we want to catch our flight."

Conor nodded, all sorts of thoughts drifting through his brain now. Telling her had probably been one of the smartest things he'd ever done.

Before they could leave the restaurant, he spied another friendly face, one he'd seen way too much of this weekend. Jacob Martin apparently needed to catch a plane, too, something Conor hadn't expected. For some reason, he'd thought the man had never left their hometown.

After shaking hands and telling each other how great it was to see all their classmates, Conor said, "I have something for you."

"Yeah?"

"Yeah. I'm pretty sure Raquel wanted to you to have this."

Jacob's eyebrows raised as Conor slipped him the folded piece of paper, and he didn't feel one inkling of guilt about it—because Raquel and Jacob belonged together a hell of a lot more than he had ever belonged with her. No...the woman he needed was by his side, just the way he hoped it would be from now on.

As they began walking down the airport terminal, a quiet calm settled over him.

Until Morgan opened her mouth.

"What did you give Jacob?"

"A happy future, I hope."

"If it's *that* good, why didn't you want to keep it?"

Kissing the top of her head, he thought about it more. "Because I have my best future right here, right now. It doesn't get any better than that."

Morgan stopped walking and pulled his face down to hers. Yes...that kiss definitely felt like the best future he ever could have imagined for himself.

Pulling luggage with their free arms, they strode hand in hand toward the boarding area. After a few minutes, Morgan said, "Since we're confessing things, I suppose I need to cop to something."

Conor had no idea what to expect and he hoped his voice didn't betray the tiny bit of fear rocking his internal organs. "What's that?"

"I lied to you when we first met. Well...maybe *embellished* is closer to the truth."

"What do you mean?"

"I, uh...I didn't have as much experience as an assistant as I'd led you to believe when I first applied for the job."

Conor couldn't help but start laughing. "Do you really think you had me fooled?"

Morgan grew quiet before she finally said, "Yeah. So if I didn't, why the hell did you hire me?"

"I liked your attitude. Even in your interview, you were a little sassy. I needed someone to keep me on my toes, and I knew my clients would love you. I tended to be all business and probably way too serious—but you changed all that. You added something to my office that was sorely missing: a spark...and you added it to my life, too."

Morgan squeezed his hand. "So you seriously knew?"

"How couldn't I, Morgan? I called your former employers and your references after I interviewed you. Trust me—I had more qualified applicants...but there was something about you, Morgan Tredway, something that told me to take a chance."

"Is that why you told me I had a six-month probation period and you could let me go at any time?"

Conor's smirk would tell her before he said the words. "Yes. But my gamble paid off. You were intuitive and willing to learn. And even though it took me a while to get used to your potty mouth in the office, I appreciated how you wanted to make yourself invaluable."

"It was 'cause I made your coffee every morning, isn't it?"

The laugh emerging from his mouth started in his belly. "That didn't hurt."

"Well...if you want to be engaged for real, maybe you'll have to start making *me* coffee. You know, woo me a little."

"That's it? You're that easy?"

"Oh, really? Mr. I'm-too-busy-to-make-coffee-for-three-hours. Let's see just how easy it is, mister. But if you want me to tack on more demands—"

"No. I'll take it."

As they found their gate and got in line, Morgan squeezed his hand. He looked down in her lovely malachite eyes and marveled that now he could gaze in them as often as he'd like. What he was about to say was going to sound sappy, but he didn't care. He rarely indulged that side of himself, but Morgan was a safe haven.

"I thought I was on top of the world, Mo. I thought I had everything a guy could want—including a spunky assistant I could also call a friend. But then this weekend, you showed me how wrong I was, how empty my life has been. I've got money, and I've got all these crazy high school memories, and it wasn't until I had you by my side that I realized I also had someone to *share* all that with. And, somehow, that's given everything meaning."

"Sir? Excuse me—*sir?*" Conor turned his head to see that the two of them were now holding up the line…so they checked in and began boarding the plane—this time not even trying to carry Morgan's luggage on board.

Once they located their seats, Conor asked, "Window or aisle?" Still willing to let Morgan have the window, he waited for her to choose.

"I don't care."

"Then I'll take the window."

They scooched inside the tight space but instead of sitting down, Conor took Morgan's hand before she could slide her purse under her seat.

"Are we really this compatible? I'm the window; you're the aisle. I'm low-key and you're spirited. I'm math and you're English."

"Oh, my God, Conor. You're sappy and I'm not."

"Exactly."

Morgan shook her head but her eyes continued to twinkle with a hidden smile. "Shut up and kiss me already. And then we need to sit down and put together a to do list."

"For our flight home?"

"No. For our engagement and wedding. You know there's a shit ton to do."

Conor laughed before doing her bidding, kissing her like it was their last, relishing the now-full space in his heart.

EPILOGUE

Morgan Tredway is with Conor Hammond
July 17 at 8:30 AM

Friends, we know this seems sudden, but Conor and I realize we belong together. We don't have an *official* date yet, but details will be forthcoming.

MESSAGE!
> **Dee Tredway-Brooks**
> Like . Reply 1m

Messenger

MON 8:33 AM

Don't you think this joke is going a little too far?

8:34 AM

No, we're serious, Dee. This is real.

8:35 AM

I thought you said this was fake for the reunion.

8:37 AM

Pretending we were engaged made us realize we should be that way for real.

8:38 AM

I suppose that makes sense. OMG. It's because you slept with him!!!

8:40 AM

That didn't hurt.

8:40 AM

You're a nut.

8:41 AM

Yeah, I know, but you love me anyway, sis.

Morgan Tredway
July 30 at 3:47 PM

Seriously…should we elope and go to Mexico for a small wedding and then have a huge reception here with food and dance or should I have the big traditional ceremony here and just have the honeymoon in Cabo? Thoughts???

You're on the clock. ;)
Conor Hammond
Like . Reply 2m

...says the guy who's checking FB. WTF?
> **Morgan Tredway**
> Like . Reply Just now

Morgan Tredway is with Conor Hammond
August 2 at 4:01 PM

Eek! Look at these rings!!! Aren't they gorgeous?

I suppose I should offer my congratulations to the two of you. But, Conor, if she's ever mean to you, you can call me. *wink*
> **Raquel Bettis**
> Like . Reply 46m

Um...babe?
> **Jacob Martin**
> Like . Reply 2m

Just kidding, teddy bear. *kisses*
> **Raquel Bettis**
> Like . Reply Just now

Morgan Tredway
August 8 at 5:59 PM

Okay, okay, okay...we finally set a date so you all would stop harassing us already. I've got a wedding planner now who's gonna kill me for the short notice, but how about November 2? That work for everybody? SAVE THE DATE ALREADY!

Conor Hammond is with Morgan (Tredway) Hammond
November 3 at 5:30 AM

Friends, it was wonderful sharing our moment together with all of you. We're at the airport right now and Morgan's already asleep in her seat, waiting for takeoff. We'll see you all next week. Thanks for celebrating with us.

I was proud to be your best man, my friend. (I warned you this would happen! lol) Now log off and start your honeymoon.
Brock Ford
Like . Reply Just now

Congratulations, guys! So glad we could be part of it!
Susan Powell
Like . Reply Just now

Morgan (Tredway) Hammond is with Conor Hammond
December 25 at 3:30 PM

First Xmas with my babe and my new in-laws! Who knew?

No pressure, but when do you plan to start a family?
Dale Hammond
Like . Reply 11m

| **Conor Hammond**

We're working on it, mom. We practice almost every night!
Like . Reply 2m

| **Morgan**

OMG TMI, **Conor**.
Like . Reply 2m

| **Steve Powell**

LOL Nope. **Dale** has that sign, remember?
Like . Reply Just now

But Conor wasn't kidding. They practiced every single night in different rooms and different positions—and they might not have had a sign to announce it, but they had a hell of a lot of fun doing it.

ACKNOWLEDGEMENTS

Greetings from Colorado!

So...I have this really bad habit. Well, not really a "habit" but something weird I do, and I don't even know I've done it till it's too late. When I'm writing a book, I oftentimes will name characters in that story similar names and not even realize it till later—and then, when I discover what I've done, I know the similarities could make for a poor reading experience (unless the characters having similar names is a plot point).

I did it with *Bullet* with two important characters and had to change one of them, and I've done it other times; I have no doubt I'll do it again!

In *Shenanigans*, I chose Morgan's name early on and loved it. It's perfect for my feisty, foul-mouthed heroine with a heart of gold—er, silver. Conor's ideal woman from high school, our villainess, perhaps, is now named Raquel, but she didn't start out that way, and that's thanks to my awesome Facebook group, Jade's Bullet Babes. When I began the editing process, it was time to fix stuff like that. My brain was tapped out, so I asked my group for good first names for a woman who is the heroine's enemy. My group didn't let me down, giving me all kinds of great suggestions.

There were sooooo many good names to choose from!

As you know, I settled on Raquel. Big thank you to Gina Marcantonio for giving me this idea. And huge thanks to these other awesome readers who also had great suggestions:

Line, Kirstyann, Lyn, Luci, Gina, Crystal, Theresa, Angie (two of you!), Mary, Jennifer, Reinta, LaDonna, Brenda, Myra, Hannah, Cathryn, Jessica, Kate, Stacy, Carrie, Melanee, Wendy, Cassie, Laurie, Shelley, Amy, Shelly, Cathy, Sarah, Mary Lou, Liz, Carole, Stephanie, Debra, Terry, and Shashauna.

Oh, and in case you're curious? Raquel's name in the first version of this book was *Marina*.

Rock on!
Jade
September 2018

BOOKS BY JADE C. JAMISON

Dream Guy

All I Want for Christmas is the Hot Guy in the Santa Suit

Picture Perfect

Heat

To Save Him

Savage

Substitute Boyfriend

Finger Bang

Quickies: Sexy Short Stories and Other Stuff

Old House

Then Kiss Me

MADversary

Laid Bare

Fabric of Night

Crossing the Line

TANGLED WEB SERIES

1 Tangled Web: A Steamy Heavy Metal Novella

2 Everything But

Punctured, Bruised, and Barely Tattooed (companion novel)

3 Seal All Exits

PRETENSE AND PROMISES SERIES

1 Charade

2 Shenanigans

BULLET SERIES

1 Bullet: An Epic Rock Star Novel

2 Rock Bottom

3 Feverish

4 Fully Automatic

4.5 Christmas Stalkings

5 Slash and Burn

6 Locked and Loaded

FEVERISH SERIES

1 Feverish

1.5 Boiling Point

2 Scorched

NICKI SOSEBEE SERIES

1 Got the Life

2 Dead

3 No Place to Hide

4 Right Now

5 One More Time

6 Lost

7 Innocent Bystander

8 Blind

9 Fake

10 Lies

11 Dead Bodies Everywhere

CODIE SNOW SERIES

1 Fool Me Once

WISHES SERIES

1 Be Careful What You Wish For

VAGABONDS TRILOGY

1 On the Run

2 On the Road

3 On the Rocks

NONFICTION

Indie Writer Companion

ABOUT THE AUTHOR

For years, Jade C. Jamison tried really hard to write what she thought was more "literary" fiction, but she found herself compelled to write what you read by her today--sometimes gritty, raw, realistic stories and other times humorous, light tales--but most of the stories she writes revolve around relationships and characters finding their way through life. While she doesn't confine herself to just one genre, nor is there a nice neat label for what she writes, most of her work could be called erotic romance. Her main writing passions include rock star romance, romantic comedy, and romantic suspense.

She lives in Colorado with her husband and four children.

Find out more at www.jadecjamison.com
Sign up for Jade's newsletter at
http://www.subscribepage.com/JadeCJamison

9 781635 765250